Susie Sneakers

SUSIE
SNEAKERS

by Scott Corbett

Illustrated by LEONARD SHORTALL

Thomas Y. Crowell Company : NEW YORK

*With love
to my daughter
Florence*

Contents

CHAPTER 1

Susie Has Her Doubts

ALL SIGNS pointed to Cape Cod. Susie Winthrop sat looking out the window of the train, and it seemed as if every sign she saw said something about Cape Cod.

She hated every one of them. She hated the thought of getting there and knowing she would have to stay all summer.

A lady sitting across the aisle spoke to her. "Is someone going to meet you?"

"Yes, my Uncle Gurney and Aunt Sally, and probably Blake and Julia, too. They're my cousins."

"Oh. Good." The lady smiled. "Have you come very far?"

"Yes, all the way from Omaha, Nebraska."

The lady looked as if she could hardly believe it. Susie did not blame her. She could hardly believe it herself.

"Why, imagine that! How old are you?"

"I'm twelve."

"Twelve years old. Well, goodness me! Did you have any trouble? I mean, like changing trains?"

"Oh, no."

"Is this your first visit to Cape Cod?"

"Yes."

"Well, well! I hope you have a good time."

"Thank you." Susie tried to smile, though her heart was not in it, and the lady went back to reading her book. Susie wondered if she should have explained that she had no trouble changing trains because she had ridden as far as New York in a car with some friends of her mother's and father's, but she was glad she had not. It was more fun to have the lady believe she had come all the way alone.

To tell the truth, though, if Susie had had her way she would never have come on the trip at all. She had hated the idea from the beginning, from the moment Aunt Sally wrote inviting her to come for the summer.

Susie had told her mother and father she did not want to go, but they had insisted that it was a wonderful opportunity for her. They told her she would love it when she got there, but Susie knew better.

She stared out the window unhappily, and then decided she was thirsty, so she got up and started down the aisle to the water fountain.

She was almost there when somebody behind her said, "Hey."

Susie turned. It was a small boy about eleven years old who was as round as he was tall. Everything about him was round. His face was round. His eyes were big and round. His button nose was round. He was chewing a piece of candy, and even his mouth was sort of going around in a circle. His hair was short and bristly, and his cheeks were apple red.

He was with his mother. Susie had heard her call him Billy. Once or twice, when she had had to scold him, she had called him Billy Snow. "Billy Snow, you sit right down in that seat!" she had said. Susie had seen them get on when the train stopped at Providence, Rhode Island, not long ago. They were sitting two seats behind her.

When Susie turned to see what Billy wanted he hurried on past her without another word. Too late she realized it was a trick to make her stop. He rushed to the water fountain and looked back at her with a chuckle. "I beat you."

"Well!" Susie frowned as he pulled a paper cup out of the cup dispenser. While she waited, he filled up the cup three times and drank noisily. Then he filled it up again and held it out to her.

"Hold that for me a second," he said, and pulled out another paper cup, the last one left in the dispenser.

Well, he *was* a funny one, Susie decided. First he was rude, and now he was going to make up for it by filling a cup for her.

When he had filled the second cup, however, he reached out and took his back from her.

"Okay," he said, and walked off down the aisle holding both cups and chuckling again.

He was taking the other cup to his mother!

"Oh, you!" cried Susie, but in a low voice—she didn't want other people to hear her and maybe laugh. She was as angry as she could be for letting him fool her—and besides that, now there were no more paper cups. She tried to figure out some way to get herself a drink, but there was no way to do it.

"Hey."

Billy Snow was back again. He held out an empty cup.

"My mother said to give you this."

"Well, all right!" Susie snatched it out of his hand. She was glad his mother had seen how rude he had been. She filled the cup and drank, while Billy stood watching solemnly.

All at once she felt water on her chin and neck and on the front of her blouse. At the same time Billy let out a whoop and went scampering off down the aisle. Susie held the cup away from her and saw that a little stream of water was trickling out of the bottom of it.

Billy Snow had poked a hole in it.

Two men started laughing, and Susie might have cried if it had not been for a lady who got up and helped her dry herself off.

"Now, wasn't that a mean trick! Boys are terrible sometimes, aren't they?" she said, but Susie could see that even she was biting her lip and trying not to laugh.

Susie went back to her seat with a red face and huddled in a corner wishing she had never heard of Cape Cod or seen a boy like Billy Snow. If he was what Cape Codders were like, she detested them already.

She turned her face to the window to hide the tears that were gathering in her eyes. She had never been so far from home before and she was miserably homesick. To make things worse, there were lots of reasons why Susie did not want to spend her summer at the seashore anyway.

For one thing, she certainly did not want to do all the things her cousins Blake and Julia had talked about when they came to Omaha for Christmas two years ago.

She did not think she would like the ocean, with all the things that swam and crawled and floated and wriggled in its vast waters.

Her mother said the seashore was fascinating, but at the same time she told Susie it was full of things you had to watch out for. Watch out for sharks, because they could bite your legs off and kill you. Watch out for turtles, because they snapped; and crabs, because they pinched; and even jellyfish, because they could sting you.

Susie liked her aunt and uncle, but she was not sure she would really have much fun with her cousins. They had not had very much fun together during their visit to Omaha.

Julia was a year younger than Susie. She had seemed like a baby in some ways and a terrible tomboy in others—though of course she had only been nine years old then. She was eleven years old now.

Blake, who was a year older than Susie, had spent most

of his time acting as if he were too big to play with girls. It would be dreadful if he acted that way all summer.

Billy Snow came back up the aisle again carrying his paper drinking cup. He made a great show of holding it up for Susie to see. It was all she could do not to stick her tongue out at him. She would also have liked to stick her foot out in the aisle to trip him. However, she remembered that she was on a train and was supposed to act like a young lady.

Billy made a silly face as he went past. He was eating candy again. Susie watched him and thought how glad she was that after they left the train she would probably never have to see him again. She wondered how big Cape Cod was. On the map it looked small, just a narrow peninsula sticking out into the ocean. It was crooked, too—in fact, it looked much the way a boy's arm looks when he bends it to show his muscle.

Billy Snow drank two more cupfuls of water very greedily and came back down the aisle. He stared at her all the way. When he got to her, he stopped and stuck his thumbs in his belt on each side of his tubby stomach.

"I know who *you* are. I saw your picture. You're Blake and Julia's cousin," he said, and marched off to his seat, leaving her with her mouth open.

CHAPTER 2

The Treasure Ship

Now, on top of everything else, Billy Snow knew her cousins! All she could hope was that he did not live near them.

She felt better when the train finally got to Cape Cod. It was not such a tiny place after all. In fact, when the train crossed the railroad bridge over the Cape Cod Canal, everything looked enormous. The canal was very broad, and on the other side of it the land extended as far as she could see. Instead of looking sandy, it was covered with trees.

A big ship was going through the canal, and that made her think about her cousin Blake.

From the way he had talked during their Christmas visit two years ago, Susie knew that Blake loved boats, especially sailboats. He still felt that way, more than ever —Aunt Sally had said so in her letters.

There was a sailboat named the *Argos* that Blake wanted more than anything else in the world. Uncle Gurney and Aunt Sally and Julia wanted it, too, because they all loved to go sailing. The man who owned the *Argos* planned to sell it, but unfortunately he wanted more money than Uncle Gurney could afford to spend. So Blake hoped to earn enough during the summer to buy it himself.

Susie wished Blake did have a sailboat, because sailing was one of the few things about Cape Cod that sounded like something she would truly enjoy. Once she had gone to a lake in Minnesota with her family and taken a ride in a boat with an outboard motor on it, and she had liked the feeling of cutting through the water in a boat.

Green fields and thick woods and neat little white houses with silvery-gray shingles went past Susie's train window. Julia and Blake had talked a lot about going out in the woods and fields for blueberries and blackberries, but Susie was afraid of the woods. In the woods you had to go places where all sorts of insects might bite you and where the grass might be full of things you could not see. You had to put your foot down in tall grass without knowing what might be there.

Susie was afraid of the seashore and the ocean and she was afraid of the woods and—well, she was just afraid. She was afraid of the outdoors. She lived in a suburb where there were no real woods around, and she was not used to such things.

The last part of the trip seemed very long. It seemed as if the train would never reach Hyannis, the town where she was supposed to get off. Susie had about given up, when the conductor stuck his cheery red face in the door of the car.

"Hyannis! Last stop! Hyannis!"

She felt a pain in her stomach, and gripped the handle of her traveling bag hard. She had kept it close to her on the seat. All the rest of her things—her hats and coats and dresses and blue jeans and sneakers and jacks and water colors—were in a big trunk that had been sent ahead on another train. She certainly hoped it had arrived safely.

She heard Billy Snow talking to the conductor, and what he was saying made her heart sink.

"You ought to see our treasure ship," he was saying. "Me and Blake have got a treasure ship."

That meant he must live near Blake, maybe even right in East Barnham!

"Got a treasure ship, eh, sonny?" The conductor laughed the way grown-ups do when they don't really believe you. But Billy was serious.

"We sure have. It's a shipwreck that got wrecked more'n a hundred years ago. We've been digging it out, and I bet we'll find some treasure."

"Well, save some for me if you do," said the conductor, still laughing.

The train went slower and slower. The station came in sight, the station platform began to slide slowly by, and then all at once—

"Susie!"

There, waving at her, were her uncle and aunt and cousins. Blake and Julia were both yelling at once. They were all walking along beside the train, keeping up with it. All except Julia, that is. Julia was jumping up and down. Her long, straight, blond hair was bouncing, and she was wild with excitement.

Julia looked much bigger than Susie had expected, and so did Blake. It seemed as if everything on Cape Cod was bigger than she had expected it to be. She knew Blake was big and strong, of course, but now he looked almost like a grown man. And Julia did not look so babyish any more, either.

Susie almost lost all hope when she looked at Blake. Now he would probably not play with them at all. Still, maybe Aunt Sally would make him, because Susie had come all the way from Omaha.

She saw him wave to Billy Snow and call out.

"Hi, Billy!"

"Hi, Blake! Hey, Ma, there's Blake, come to fetch his cousin. Hey, there's Pa! Come on, let's get going." Billy dragged his mother up the aisle before Susie could even think of getting up.

When she finally jumped down from the train they were all waiting, and the whole family hugged and kissed her. All except Blake, that is. He had to be told to kiss her, and then he only gave her a quick peck on the cheek. Blake considered kissing sissy stuff.

"Alma and Josh, this is Susie Winthrop. Susie, this is Mr. and Mrs. Snow—and this is Billy," said Aunt Sally, and Susie found herself being introduced to Billy and his parents.

"How do you do?" she said to his parents, but she only

glared at him. Billy laughed and danced a little jig. He was so fat that he reminded Susie of a rubber ball bouncing up and down. He was glad to be home, even though he had been away for only a couple of days.

While the grown-ups were talking, Blake edged over to Billy and whispered to him. "Hey, Billy, did you get them?"

Billy nodded. "Yep."

"Get what?" cried Julia, who never missed much.

"Never mind," said Blake, looking very wise and mysterious. "Just something we wanted."

"Tell me!"

"None of your business, nosey."

"Mommy, Blake and Billy have a secret and won't tell," cried Julia, tugging at Aunt Sally's sleeve.

"Well, I suppose that's their privilege," said Aunt Sally. "Why don't you girls have a secret, too?"

"Shall we have a secret, Susie?"

"Yes." But like Julia, Susie still wanted to know what the boys' secret was. What had Billy Snow brought back that was so important?

While they were still wondering, Blake thought of something else.

"Hey, Billy, where's Caroline?"

"Ma wouldn't let me take her along."

"Oh."

Susie wondered who Caroline was, and decided she must be Billy Snow's dog—probably a poor little dog that Billy tormented all day long. Before she could ask, Aunt Sally said, "Blake, take Susie's bag for her. Well, dear, how does it seem to be here?"

Susie swallowed hard. She wondered what to say.

"Well . . ."

Aunt Sally laughed, and squeezed her hand.

"Never mind—you've hardly had a chance to find out yet. Come on, let's all go home to supper."

The Snows got into a small truck. Billy scrambled up to ride in the back. He waved and grinned a saucy grin as the truck went rolling off down the road. He was standing up, hanging on to the side; and it annoyed Susie to think that a pest like Billy Snow should have all that fun. Uncle

Gurney's station wagon was nice, but certainly not as much fun as a truck.

Pine woods lined the road on both sides as they rode home. It was getting close to dusk, and the woods looked gloomy. Susie was glad to be snug in the car, sitting in the back seat with Julia on one side of her and Tina on the other. Tina was the family dog. She was a beagle. She was fat, but she had a nice face and was smart and friendly.

They all asked Susie questions about her trip—all except Tina, of course—and Julia asked twice as many as anybody else. Julia made her feel really welcome. First she would hold her hand, then she would hug her, and then she would squeal with excitement or giggle in her funny way that made everybody else laugh, too.

"Susie, guess what?" she said finally, clapping her hands together.

Blake, who was sitting on the other side of Julia and acting very grown-up, now leaned forward and frowned fiercely at his sister.

"All right, Julia! Don't tell her yet!"

"But I've *got* to, Blake."

"You don't have to do any such a thing."

"I can't stand it!"

"Oh, let her tell, Blake," said Aunt Sally.

"Aw, gee whiz, Mom, I don't see why we can't save it for a special surprise."

Uncle Gurney laughed. "Well, you can't very well not tell Susie now, after making her this curious. At least, I suppose you're curious, aren't you, Susie?"

"Yes, Uncle Gurney."

"Heck, I don't see why Julia's always got to blab everything," growled Blake, and gave his sister a slap on the arm. He had to lean across Susie to do it, and when he did his elbow dug into Susie's stomach.

"Oof!"

" 'Scuse me, Susie. Well, anyway, what happened is that—"

"We had a big storm last week and it washed a lot of sand away on one part of the beach and uncovered an old shipwreck!" cried Julia before Blake could go on. Blake dived across at his sister and poor Susie, being in the middle, got all the worst of it. Tina jumped down on the floor to get out of the way, and for a moment Susie felt like jumping down there with her.

"I know all about it," she cried. "I heard Billy Snow tell the conductor on the train about it."

Luckily that made them stop fighting. Their faces fell.

"Oh, darn him!" said Julia.

"Wait till I get that squash-head!" growled Blake. "I suppose he had to blab everything!"

"No, all he said was that you had a treasure ship and it was a shipwreck over a hundred years old."

"Well, not quite *that* old," said Uncle Gurney, chuckling.

"That's all he told you, then?" Blake sounded relieved. "Well, anyway—"

"Didn't he—"

"You shut up now, Julia, and let *me* tell some of it."

"Blake, it isn't nice to say 'shut up.'"

"Well, gee, Mom—"

"There. You see?" said Julia primly. "Well, this shipwreck—"

"Now, wait a minute, Julia," said her mother. "Blake is right, even though he did say 'shut up.' You must be quiet and let him have a turn."

"But, Mommy, I was only going to tell Susie about the—"

"Julia!" said Uncle Gurney.

"Oh, darn it, Daddy," grumbled Julia, "I never get to do anything, like just tell a little bit about the ribs and how they—"

"You cut that out!" cried Blake.

At that point Uncle Gurney took one hand off the steering wheel. He took his pipe out of his mouth. He drew in a deep breath. And he spoke very loudly.

"QUIET!"

Everybody was quiet.

Uncle Gurney glanced over his shoulder, looking so

stern that he reminded Susie of her school principal back
home.

"Now, then. Blake, you may go ahead. And Julia, if we
hear one more word from you, you will go to bed right
after supper."

Blake leaned forward, looking very pleased.

"Well, after the big storm Billy Snow went down to the
beach to see if the high tide had washed anything good
up onto the shore. He was walking along down near
Howes Point where the bluff is high, and the tide had
chewed a big hunk out of it. And sticking out of the sand
in front of it was a bunch of big curved boards. They
looked like the ribs of some prehistoric monster."

"But they were really part of a ship?"

"Yes. An old sailing ship."

"Long ago, when a ship was wrecked and parts of it
washed ashore, the sand gradually covered up those parts,"
said Uncle Gurney. "Then, sometimes years later and
sometimes hundreds of years later, a big storm such as we
had the other day washes out a part of the beach where a
wreck is buried and uncovers it. Every now and then that
happens along the shore."

"You mean the beach isn't the same all the time?"
asked Susie, who felt startled to think it could change
that much. "You mean it moves?"

Uncle Gurney nodded.

"It certainly does, all the time. The sea wears it away in one place and builds it up in another. Sometimes after a big storm there's a whole new sandbar built up somewhere."

"We've been digging sand away from the wreck so as to uncover more of it," Blake said importantly, "and we hope that maybe we'll be able to find something that will tell us what ship it was. Mr. Snow thinks it's the *Island Gull*, that was wrecked clear back in the great storm of '98. That's nearly sixty years ago."

Julia wanted to talk so badly she could hardly stand it. She kept waving her hand as if she were in school, but she did not dare say anything. She knew her father meant what he said about what would happen if she did.

"We uncovered the stump of one of the masts, and it's that big around." Blake held his arms in a great huge circle. "Wait till you see."

"All right, Julia. I see you waving," said Uncle Gurney. "Now you may say something."

"Oh, great," said Julia disgustedly. "What is there left to tell? He's already told about the mast."

"Then next time don't try to be the whole show and you may do better," said Uncle Gurney. "Well, Susie, we're getting close to home. This is East Barnham now."

CHAPTER 3

Things from the Sea

THEY DROVE past a drugstore and filling station and grocery, passed several big white houses, and turned off the highway into a little village.

The houses there were not as close together as the houses at home, but they were not far apart, either. In the middle of the village a white church steeple rose above the trees.

The streets were lined with tall elms and horse-chestnut trees, and the flowers in the yard were brilliant dots of pure color. Susie loved flowers, and it seemed to her she had never seen any so bright. In the soft light of dusk some of the red flowers seemed almost to glow.

Near the edge of the little village they came to a big white house with silver-gray shingles. They turned into the driveway and stopped. Tina got down on the floor and stood with her nose against the car door waiting to get out.

"Here we are," cried Julia. "Come on, Susie, I'll show you my room. You're going to be with me."

"Blake, you and I will carry in Susie's trunk," said Uncle Gurney—for the trunk had been waiting at the station, safe and sound.

Julia raced ahead and held open the back door, dancing up and down with impatience for Susie to hurry and come see her room. They went in through the big kitchen and upstairs to a room which had a sign written with crayons hanging on the door. The sign said:

Quiet.
HOSTPITIL
Please Do Not Enter.

"You spelled hospital wrong," said Susie, and spelled it correctly for Julia.

"Oh, well, we'll make a new sign. Look, Susie, here's my bed and here's where you're going to sleep. Daddy brought your bed down from the attic."

There were two beds exactly alike in the room. Susie felt that pain in her stomach again when she thought about living all summer in a strange room. Julia's clothes and toys were all over the place in a helter-skelter fashion. The real trouble with the room was that it had a very odd smell about it. Susie sniffed and wrinkled up her nose.

"What is that awful smell?"

"Oh! Close the door," said Julia, and quickly did it herself, quietly and mysteriously. She went to her closet and crawled in on her hands and knees. Muffled by the clothes hanging in the closet, her voice sounded far away.

"Wait till you see what I found today."

She backed out, pulling a big box along the floor. Immediately the odd smell became stronger. It did not seem to bother Julia, however. She reached in the box and brought out a strange, five-pointed star that was dark-colored and had bumps all over it. From pictures she had seen in books, Susie guessed at once what it must be.

"Is that a starfish?"

"Yes."

"Is it *alive?*"

"It was when I pulled it off a rock this morning. I guess it isn't now, though. I'm going to let it dry out. If you let them dry you can keep them forever, or anyway for a long, long time. Here, want to see it?"

Susie hesitated, and then touched the starfish with one finger. It felt hard, and she could not imagine its ever being alive. She thought perhaps that Julia only pretended it was alive—or maybe Blake had told her it was, to fool her.

"And look what else I found."

Susie got down on her knees beside Julia, to look in the
box. She saw some strange-looking shells, one white and
one blue.

"This blue one is a mussel, and the white one is a clam.
See the clam's neck sticking out?"

Sure enough, a part of the clam was sticking out of the
shell.

"Is that a sea clam?"

"Oh, no. They're big. This is a soft-shelled clam."

"Is *it* alive?"

"Oh, sure." Julia touched the neck of the clam with her
finger, and it drew in its neck and closed its shell tightly.

Susie's eyes grew round. "Why, it really is. Is the blue one alive, too—the whatchamacallit?"

"The mussel? Yes, but mussels are different. You can't make a mussel *do* anything."

The door opened and Aunt Sally came in, followed by Blake and Uncle Gurney carrying Susie's trunk. In a flash Julia shoved the box back in the closet, but it was too late to do anything about the smell. She could not hide that.

Aunt Sally sniffed. "Julia! What have you got in this room?"

Julia sighed. "I guess maybe it's my starfish."

"Your starfish? Do you mean to tell me you've got that starfish up here? You're to leave that out in the sun to dry, do you hear me?"

"Well, I forgot to, and now there's no sun, Mommy."

"There will be in the morning, and in the meantime you put it out on the back porch. What else is in that box?"

"Just a clam and a mussel."

"A clam and a mussel? I suppose they're dead, too."

"I should say not! Are they, Susie?"

"Oh, no, Aunt Sally. The clam pulled its neck in and shut up its shell."

"Nevertheless, I want that whole box of things to go out on the back porch. Why, this room smells like the clam flats at low tide." Aunt Sally looked around the room and then scolded Julia. "I thought I told you to straighten up this room and put things away before we left for the station. It's a disgrace. You haven't even cleared out that corner for Susie's trunk. Now you get busy."

For a few minutes, Aunt Sally made things fly. Especially she made Julia fly. Dresses were hung up in the closet, toys disappeared into drawers, books slid into place on bookshelves, and the room began to look almost neat.

There was a chest of drawers in one corner of the room. Susie's aunt showed her an empty drawer she could put her clothes in.

"Now, you can help Susie unpack, Julia, and then I want both of you to come downstairs, because supper will soon be ready."

After Susie's trunk had been set in its corner, Blake picked up something from Julia's dressing table.

"Hey, this is my bluefish jaw."

Julia flew at him, but he held it out of reach.

"Blake, it is not! You gave it to me."

"I did not."

"You did so."

"Not for keeps, I didn't."

"Blake," said his father. "Don't be an Indian giver."

Blake tried not to look sheepish. He handed the bluefish jaw to Julia. "Aw, all right. I can always get plenty more," he said, and swaggered out of the room.

"Aw, I can get plenty more, too," mimicked Uncle

Gurney, and swaggered out exactly the way Blake had. It was so much like him that even Blake had to grin.

"Aw, cut it out, Dad!"

When the girls were alone, Susie looked curiously at the bluefish jaw.

"Is that a real fish's jaw?"

"Yes. Feel the teeth."

"All right. Ow!"

It seemed to Susie she had barely touched the teeth, and yet they had stuck her.

"They're terribly sharp," said Julia. "Bluefish can give you a real bad bite. You have to be careful taking them off the hook."

"You won't catch *me* taking any of them off any hook," said Susie, sucking her finger.

"Oh, but it's fun to go fishing."

Susie got the key to her trunk out of her traveling bag and opened it up. Right on top were two of her nicest, frilliest dresses. Her mother had put them there so that nothing would crush them.

"Oh, what lovely dresses! But you won't need them hardly ever," said Julia, grabbing them and tossing them aside on the bed.

"Julia, don't! I have to hang them right up." Susie picked them up and smoothed them out. Then she got hangers out of the closet and hung them up carefully.

While she was doing it, Julia investigated her trunk some more.

"Blue jeans . . . sneakers . . . sweaters . . . a jacket. Good. You'll need all those. And what's this? Oh—a beach ball. That's good."

Susie looked around the room, and it began to seem as though everything in it was strange and spoke of the sea. Sitting on Julia's dressing table were two big sea shells, and in each shell were dozens of small blue, brown, white, and pink shells Julia had collected.

Hanging on the wall was a painted shell with a long, spiky tail sticking out from under it; and in another place a huge red claw hung by a string from a thumbtack.

Between the windows were two framed pictures of sailboats. Even the window curtains spoke of the sea. They were made of fish net.

"You must really like the ocean, Julia."

"I love it. Wait till you see it, you'll love it, too. Here, put this conch shell against your ear, and you can hear how the ocean sounds," said Julia, picking up a big, twisted shell. Susie put it to her ear and listened to a far-off, mysterious, roaring sound. She was fascinated, but she was uneasy, too, because there was so much she did not know about the ocean.

"Well, let's go downstairs and see when supper will be ready," said Julia. "I'm hungry!"

Caroline

"Do we have to set the table?" asked Julia.

"No, not tonight. You and Blake can go out and show Susie around a little. That will take your minds off your stomachs until dinner is ready. Go show her the barn."

The barn, where the car was kept, was much bigger than a regular garage. There was room enough for two more cars if Uncle Gurney had owned them. Instead he had his garden tools and bags of grass seed and fertilizer there. There was a big loft upstairs.

Everything was different from Susie's home. The house was not so different, but everything around it was. There were woods alongside the barn. Behind the house and the barn the ground sloped off down to a gully with trees and bushes growing thickly in it. On the other side of the gully a wide flat marsh stretched away in all directions.

It was a long way to the highway and the hills on the other side.

"Are there animals in those woods, Blake?"

"Oh, sure. Deer come through here all the time, and lots of small animals like woodchucks and rabbits and skunks. One night I opened the garage door for Dad—"

"And a fox ran out!" cried Julia. This time Blake did not get mad. Maybe it was because he had so much fun telling about the shipwreck while Julia had to be quiet.

"A fox?" Susie decided then and there never to be the one to open the garage door at night for her uncle. She did not want any fox running out at *her*. "What did it do to you?"

"Do to me?" Blake laughed. "It didn't do anything, silly. It ran away as fast as it could. I'd have caught it, only I was too surprised to grab it."

"You would not have caught it," said Julia. "Daddy said a fox can bite you very badly."

"Well, just the same, I wouldn't have been scared to grab it, if I could have got it by the neck," bragged Blake.

Before Susie could ask any more questions about the fox, he began to talk about his favorite subject—the *Argos*. He never quite stopped thinking about the sailboat, it seemed, no matter what he was doing.

"Tomorrow I'll take you down to the harbor for a look at the *Argos*. There isn't a finer sailboat in the whole bay.

And guess what? Mr. McGill at the boat shop is going to let me work for him every morning, starting next week, and he's going to pay me ten dollars a week. And besides that I've got three lawns to mow every week. I get two dollars apiece for those. So maybe I'll be able to buy her after all."

"Oh, that would be wonderful!"

For a minute Blake was happy, but then his face lost its glow. He sat down on an old barrel with his elbows on his knees and his chin resting on his fists. He looked discouraged.

"Only trouble is, there's a man that's offered Mr. Cartwright four hundred dollars for her. Four hundred dollars! And Mr. Cartwright wants to sell her at the end of the summer season, right after Labor Day. That's twelve weeks from next week, when I start working for Mr. McGill at the boat shop."

"Twelve weeks times ten dollars is a hundred and twenty dollars," said Julia, "and twelve times six dollars for mowing three lawns is seventy-two dollars, and that makes a hundred and ninety-two dollars in all. I ought to know—Blake has figured it up twenty times."

"Well, anyway," said Blake, "that's still not enough. I've got to figure out some way to make some more money, or Mr. Schenley will get the *Argos* instead of me." Blake looked miserable just thinking about it.

"That old Mr. Schenley." Julia kicked a stick across the barn floor. "He's really goony."

"Mr. Cartwright has promised me first chance to buy the *Argos*, but if I don't have the money then Mr. Schenley will buy it—and he doesn't have to worry about money at all. He's rich."

"Gee, I wish I could help."

A screen door slammed on a house that stood down the road a little way on the other side.

"Here comes Billy Snow, I'll bet," said Julia.

Now it was Susie's turn to feel bad. "Billy Snow?" She all but groaned. "Does he live that near to you?"

"Sure."

"He must have Caroline with him," said Julia. "He's walking. You can always tell when Billy has Caroline with him, because then he never runs. Running bothers Caroline. Besides, he might fall and hurt her."

"Who's Caroline?"

"You'll see," said Blake.

"Caroline is just lovely," said Julia.

"But what about Billy? Do you really like Billy, Blake?"

"Sure, Billy's all right."

"Do you like him, Julia?"

"Yes. He's funny."

"Well, I can tell you one thing, I don't like him," Susie burst out. "He was a mean little brat on the train.

He made me spill water down the front of my dress and everything."

"He did? How did he do that?"

"Hey, Billy, did you make Susie spill water on her dress on the train?" asked Blake as Billy turned into the driveway. Billy grinned.

"I didn't know she was your cousin."

"You said you did!" Susie reminded him hotly.

"That was after. I'm sorry, let's shake hands," said Billy, and took hold of her hand. "Ever see this?"

He took her fingers one at a time, beginning with the thumb, and said a word with each one.

"This—little—kitty—went—me-e-e—"

"Ow!" yelled Susie, because as he reached her last finger he gave it a good bend.

"That's right—meow!" said Billy, and suddenly his round face split into a big grin and he laughed so hard he shook all over. Susie tried to kick him in the shins but missed. Blake made a grab for him and got him.

"Hey, that's a good trick, let me try it on you," he said, but Billy got away by yelling, "Look out, you might hurt Caroline."

Blake let him go.

"Where is she?"

Billy touched his pocket. "Right here."

"Show her to Susie."

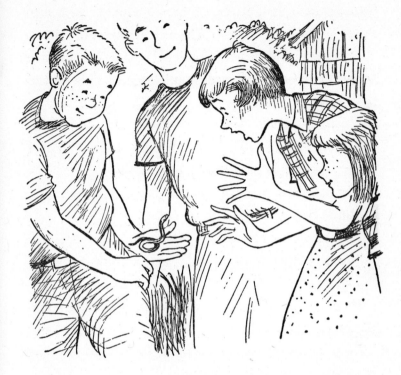

"Okay. Come here, Caroline," said Billy, reaching in his pocket and pulling out—

"A *snake!*" screamed Susie. She threw up her hands and ran away as fast as she could to the house. She burst into the kitchen and ran past her surprised Aunt Sally, crying as she went, and did not stop until she was up in Julia's room on her bed.

Caroline was actually a small green grass snake, not ten inches long. She was a gentle creature and completely harmless. When Susie threw up her hands, she frightened poor Caroline half to death. She scrambled back into Billy's pocket even faster than Susie had run for the house.

"Oh, gee!" said Blake. "Now we'll get the dickens from Mom. We'd better go inside and tell her we didn't mean to scare Susie, I guess."

"Imagine, being scared of Caroline," said Julia. "Mommy's going to be mad, all right. I don't think I want to go in right now, unless we have to."

The back door opened.

"Julia! Blake!"

"I guess we have to."

"Your mother sounds mad," agreed Billy Snow. "I think I'll go home."

He pulled his pocket open and looked down in it. "You all right, Caroline?"

Caroline seemed to be all right, so Billy went home and Blake and Julia went inside.

Up in Julia's room, Susie was lying on her bed sobbing and wishing she had never seen Cape Cod, where there were woods too close to the house and barns with foxes running out of them and nasty fat boys with snakes in their pockets. All she wished was that she could get back on a train and go home and never return again.

The whole family came upstairs and her cousins said they were sorry about scaring her. At the same time, Aunt Sally did not scold them as much as Susie had expected.

"I know it must have startled you, but you really shouldn't be afraid of Caroline, dear. She's really the most harmless little creature in the world."

"Caroline is my favorite serpent," admitted Uncle Gurney. "She has personality. Always remember that there are no poisonous snakes on Cape Cod, Susie. None of them here could hurt you seriously, even if they bit you, which isn't likely. And a tiny one like Caroline can't bite you at all—not that she would if she could. Caroline is too much of a lady."

Aunt Sally patted Susie's shoulder. "I know you're worried about being here, dear, but I think you'll learn to like it," she said gently. "Just give Cape Cod a chance."

"Sure, tomorrow we'll have a lot of fun!" cried Blake. "Don't forget—tomorrow I'm going to take you down to the harbor to see the *Argos*."

The way he said it, you would have thought that made up for everything.

CHAPTER 5

The Argos

"You have good long legs, Susie; you can use my bicycle," said Aunt Sally.

It was a nice blue bike, and Susie found she could handle it without trouble. She pedaled along through the village behind her cousins, past big white houses and neat cottages. Blake pointed out big houses he said were called captain's houses and some smaller ones that were called mate's houses. In the days of the great clipper ships, and even before, the captains and first mates had built the houses and lived in them.

All the yards had flowers blooming in them—red and pink roses, purple and yellow and scarlet tulips, and huge blue hydrangeas. Last night they had seemed to glow softly. Today, in the sunlight, their colors were dazzling.

"Well, that's *one* nice thing about Cape Cod, at least," she said to herself rather grumpily as she rode along.

Presently they turned a corner and the road rolled away in front of them down a long hill toward the blue waters of the bay. At the end of the road a small harbor crowded with dories and dinghies and sailboats sparkled in the sunshine. Rowboats were pulled up on its beaches, and a dozen sailboats were moored out in the middle. Their sails were down, and the bare masts swung gently as the boats rocked in a fair breeze that was sending a ripple of choppy waves up the harbor. Out past the boats, where the channel led to open water, jetties extended into the bay, protecting the harbor like two stone arms.

Blake pointed. "There's the *Argos*."

"Which one?"

"She's that terrific one right in the middle."

At that distance one sailboat looked exactly like another to Susie. She had no idea which one he meant. It was easy to see, though, that one of them had a special look as far as Blake was concerned. He seemed to become excited at the very sight of it. His voice shook, and his eyes gleamed.

"Come on, let's go. I'll row you across to the boat shop. I've got to see Mr. McGill and find out if I'm sure going to start work next Saturday."

When they reached the harbor, Blake and Julia both took off their sneakers and waded out to pull a boat in to the edge of the shore.

"Is that Uncle Gurney's rowboat?"

"It's his dory," said Blake. "That's what this kind is called, a dory."

Just then Susie looked in the water where Julia was standing and let out a gasp. She saw two crabs in the water beside Julia's bare feet.

"Julia! There's two crabs right beside you!"

Julia looked down and wiggled her bare toes at them. They scuttled away.

"They're just little ones. They don't even nip, that kind."

"Okay, get in," Blake ordered in his ship commander's voice, and Susie scrambled meekly up over the bow of the boat behind Julia and sat down on a seat—a "thwart," Blake called it. He shoved the boat out into the water and swung himself in over the side. He put the oars in the oar-locks and started rowing.

"I want to row," said Julia.

"You can row coming back."

"All right, you remember, now." Julia pointed ahead of them. "Look, Susie. There's the *Argos*."

Now that they were closer, Susie could see what a beautiful boat it was. Slim and graceful, the *Argos* sat on the water as light as a bird, with the sunshine gleaming on her dark polished wood and her rigging humming in the breeze. Her single mast looked tall and proud. Once again

Blake got that hungry, longing expression on his face.

"She'd really skim along today. Wind's just right."

"Have you ever had a ride in her, Blake?"

"Yes. So's Julia. Mr. Cartwright's taken me out with him three times and even let me sail her part of the time we were out."

"I've only been once, and then not for very long," grumbled Julia.

"Well, I haven't ever been out for very long in her, either."

As she looked at the *Argos*, Susie began to understand how Blake felt.

"Gee, I wish we could figure out some way to earn some more money," said Julia. "Maybe if Susie and I ran a lemonade stand—"

"Huh! You can't make much with lemonade," said Blake. "If only our treasure ship would turn out to *be* a treasure ship! Tomorrow Billy and I are going to go dig some more around it."

"I want to go, too," cried Julia.

"Well, maybe, if you don't make a pest of yourself."

As they neared the opposite bank, Julia said, "There's Mr. Cartwright in the boat shop now, talking to Mr. McGill."

Blake, working the oars, paused between strokes and glanced over his shoulder. He nodded.

"Yes, that's him. Golly, I wish I could walk right up to him and say, 'Here, Mr. Cartwright, here's your money. Now, come September, the *Argos* is mine.'"

"Why is he waiting until September to sell her?"

"Because he wants to use her himself as long as he's here. He works in Boston, but his company is going to move him to Denver this fall. I wonder what he's doing here now, though? He usually only comes down week ends. Maybe his vacation has started."

Blake ran the prow of the boat up onto the shore. He and Julia quickly jumped over the side into the shallow water and pulled it up. Blake took the anchor out of the front of the boat, carried it up the beach a few feet, and stuck it into the sand.

At the water's edge in front of the boat shop there was a dock with a gas pump standing on it, like the ones at filling stations. Boats came there to get gas for their motors. The shop itself was a long, low building, with boats up on wooden rests alongside it. Inside the shop Mr. McGill was repairing the hull of a catboat.

When the children climbed the bank, the men looked around at them and nodded.

"Well, here comes my junior assistant," said Mr. Mc-Gill. "And Julia. Hello, Julia. And I suppose this is that cousin from Omaha you said was coming?"

Mr. McGill was a small, wiry man with a tanned and

wrinkled face and a twinkle in his squinting eyes. Susie liked him, even though he made her feel self-conscious when he started talking about "that cousin from Omaha."

"Ready to go to work, Blake?"

"I sure am, Mr. McGill."

The other man chuckled. Mr. Cartwright was a big, heavy-set man with a ruddy face. He was chewing on a cigar.

"I hope you're going to pay him enough so he can buy the *Argos*, Mac. I'd like to sell it to the lad."

Mr. McGill rubbed his chin and looked as if he wished he could, too. But he shook his head.

"Afraid I won't be able to do that, much as I'd like to see him have it."

"I hate to sell that boat." Mr. Cartwright wagged his big head sadly and chewed his cigar from one side of his mouth to the other. "I've had her for many and many a year. Don't think I'd have much use for her out in Denver, though. Sensible thing is to sell her, and that's that."

"Are you on your vacation now, Mr. Cartwright?"

"No, Blake, I just had a chance to sneak down here for a couple of extra days. Got to come every chance I get, before I head for Colorado." He looked down at the three of them and grinned. "So this is your cousin from Omaha, hey? Well, we ought to show her a good time, so she'll like it here. I don't suppose you'd like to take her for a sail, say for an hour? I'm going to take some friends out, but not till this afternoon."

Blake's eyes grew round. He was almost trembling.

"Gee, do you mean it, Mr. Cartwright? You mean, I can take the *Argos* out alone?"

"Sure, why not? You're a good sailor; I know I can trust her with you."

It sounded like heaven on earth, even to Susie. Just the

three of them, sailing in the *Argos* on a day like this! They exchanged delighted glances, and Blake looked back at Mr. Cartwright.

"Gee, that's swell of you, Mr. Cartwright! Thanks a lot!" Blake was so eager to get started that he wasted not a second. "Well, let's get going, you girls, and—"

Before they could go, however, another man walked into the boat shop. He strutted in with all the self-importance of a turkey, and he reminded Susie of one. He was a short man with a good-sized pot belly, pale eyes with little pouches under them, and a sandy mustache that hardly looked worth raising. He was smoking a large pipe. He had on a yachting cap and a blue coat with brass buttons on it, as if he might be the captain of a boat. The coat and cap looked very new. They looked more like a costume than something he was used to wearing.

"Well! Hello, Henry. Hello, Mac," he said, showing large, irregular teeth around the sides of the pipe.

Mr. McGill nodded, and Mr. Cartwright said, "Hi, Beemis. Blake, here's the man who's going to buy the *Argos*. This is Mr. Beemis Schenley. Beemis, this is the boy I was telling you about that has first chance at my boat —if he can get the money up."

"Oh, yeah?" Mr. Schenley took his pipe out of his mouth and stopped to have a good look at Blake. "Well, take it easy, kid, and give me a chance," he said, with a big wink and a smirk at Mr. Cartwright. "I want that boat."

Blake looked down at the ground, not knowing what to say, as Mr. Schenley let out a heavy laugh.

"The kids were just leaving to go for a sail," said Mr. Cartwright. "I told Blake he could take the *Argos* for an hour."

"Yeah? Say, that sounds like a good idea, I think I'll go along," said Mr. Schenley. "It's a great day for it."

"Well, that's up to Blake," said Mr. Cartwright, looking as though he wished he had not mentioned it. But Mr. Schenley did not notice how long Blake's face had become.

"Okay, let's go," he said noisily, slapping Blake on the back. "I hear you like to sail, kid. You play your cards right with me and maybe I'll take you for a ride sometime, after I own the boat."

Mr. Schenley strutted out of the shop with the three children following along silently behind him. Blake looked as if the world had fallen in on him, and Susie felt awful herself. Their wonderful sail in the *Argos* was spoiled. Of all the people to have butt in, it had to be the very man who wanted to buy the boat. And then to have him turn out to be a man like Mr. Schenley made it just that much worse.

CHAPTER 6

Trouble with Mr. Schenley

"You got a rowboat here? That it? Okay, let's hop in and get going. I haven't too much time." Mr. Schenley stepped awkwardly into the boat, which teetered under his weight. He sat down in the stern and the girls huddled together in the bow while Blake rowed them out to the *Argos*. Mr. Schenley climbed aboard the sailboat and settled himself comfortably on one of the side seats.

"You can get her going and sail her for a while, my boy, and then I'll take over. I want to see what she can do today." Blake went silently to work, getting the boat ready to go. The girls sat down across from the man.

Mr. Schenley cocked his eye up at the mast and nodded.

"She's a trim little craft, all right," he said, and knocked his pipe ashes out on the gunwale. He banged his pipe on the rail and the hot ashes fell out on the wood.

"Gee, you're liable to burn the varnish that way, Mr. Schenley," Blake burst out, horrified.

"Didn't hurt it any," said the man, brushing the ashes off into the water. "All this dark, polished wood is a nuisance anyway. When I get her I'll slap a coat of white paint on her and then I'll have something."

"White p-paint?" Blake looked sick at the thought.

"Sure. I always did want a white boat," said Mr. Schenley, leaning back and filling his lungs with air. He was like a lot of grown-ups. He was so busy thinking about himself that he never noticed what the children seemed to be thinking.

Blake gulped and set his jaw. He cast off, hoisted the mainsail, sprang to the tiller, and steered them smoothly down the channel. When they were clear of the channel and the jetty and in open water he told Julia to hold the tiller, and went forward and broke out the jibsail.

The *Argos* tipped a little as the sails filled with air, and she went cutting through the water with none of that push and effort that Susie had felt in the motorboat. There was no noise, either. It was a wonderful feeling to be sailing along, and Susie could understand now why Blake felt the way he did about the *Argos*. The boat seemed to do exactly what he wanted her to do.

"Isn't this super?" whispered Julia. Susie nodded. If only they could have been alone, it would have been perfect. Even with Mr. Schenley there, Blake looked happy as he sat holding the tiller. In fact, he looked as if he had forgotten all about the man, just as the man had forgotten all about him.

For a long time nobody said anything. They just sailed. Mr. Schenley rolled up his pants legs and sat back with his arms stretched along the gunwale on each side of him, humming and drumming on the wood with his fingers. Finally he stirred around.

"Oh, red sails in the sunset, 'way out on the sea . . ." he sang in a loud and somewhat cracked voice, and then turned and started edging back along the seat. "Okay, sonnie, I'll take over for a while now. Keep your heads down, girls—I'm going to bring her around and start beating back to windward."

Without a word, Blake yielded the tiller and sat down across from the girls where the man had been sitting. Blake's head was down. Susie felt very sorry for him.

Mr. Schenley took hold of the tiller with sort of a grab, as though he did not intend to take any nonsense from the *Argos*, but meant to show her who was boss.

"Okay, here we go," he said. He bore hard on the tiller, bringing the *Argos* around to head back in the other direction, but at an angle.

"Now we have to tack," Julia told Susie. "When you tack, that means you have to sail in a zigzag. That's the only way you can make the boat travel against the wind. Isn't that right, Blake?"

"Uh-huh," said Blake. He felt too bad to talk much. He shoved his hands deep in his pockets and hunched down in his seat, staring out ahead of them. If he had not been Blake, Susie would have sworn he had tears in his eyes. Maybe it was just from the wind blowing in his face, she decided.

As soon as Mr. Schenley took over sailing her, the *Argos* began to balk. Her sails slatted, flapping and snapping violently in the wind, and she wallowed around instead of moving along smoothly.

"Doggone it, what's the matter with this fool craft?" snapped the man. He was struggling with the ropes and the tiller and getting red in the face. Susie didn't know anything about boats, but she watched and began to suspect that maybe the trouble was with Mr. Schenley. Perhaps he was not a very good sailor, though certainly he thought he was. Anybody could see that.

Blake sat right where he was, even though it was plain that he was itching to take over and get the *Argos* straightened out. But you could tell that Mr. Schenley would not accept any help if it had been offered. He wanted to show the boat who was boss.

"Settle down, darn you, settle down!" he cried, yanking on the ropes that controlled the sails. The blocks creaked and the ropes creaked and the *Argos* acted as cranky as an old horse.

"Oh, the heck with it, I'll come around again and we'll sail down a little farther. I guess we've got time before we have to turn back," he snapped, and swung the tiller around hard again, to head back the way they had been going. He was standing up a little, holding the ropes, when he did it. Blake let out a warning cry.

"Duck, Mr. Schenley!"

He yelled just in time. The boom that held the lower part of the sail was swinging over above their heads, and Mr. Schenley had forgotten to duck. He pulled his head down as Blake yelled. The boom missed his head but hit the top of his jaunty yachting cap and knocked it right over the side into the water.

"Hey! My cap!" cried Mr. Schenley, feeling his head, which turned out to be very bald. "Hey, turn back! I mean—"

In his excitement he forgot for an instant that he was running the boat himself. When he did remember, he pulled on the tiller again, hard.

"Duck!" yelled Blake again, and again just in time. Mr. Schenley almost fell flat in the bottom of the boat this time as he got his head down out of the way.

All the children were trying hard not to laugh, and Susie and Blake might have managed all right if it had not been for Julia. Julia was a giggler. When something struck her funny she had to laugh. And when she saw Mr. Schenley down on his hands and knees in the bottom of the boat, it was too much for Julia.

"Gee, Mr. Schenley!"

Still on his hands and knees, he whirled his red face in her direction. With his chin sticking out and his teeth showing, he looked exactly like a bulldog.

"What's *your* trouble?" he asked, trying to be very sarcastic.

"I'm s-sorry!" stammered Julia, choking with laughter.

She was too much for the others. They started laughing, too. They could not help themselves. They rolled around on the seats, laughing, while Mr. Schenley used some bad language and struggled to get the boat going back to where he lost his cap.

It would not go. No matter how he tried, he could not seem to get the *Argos* pointed at his cap. He zigged and he zagged, but he always ended up in the wrong place. Finally Blake staggered weakly to his feet and made himself stop laughing.

"Let me handle her and you crawl out on the bow and be ready to grab your cap, sir," he said. Mr. Schenley did not look pleased; but still he did want to get his yachting cap back, so he growled "okay" and went forward and crawled out on the front of the boat on his stomach. This was not easy with a stomach the size of Mr. Schenley's, but he managed.

"Okay, now do as I tell you," he called over his shoulder. "Bear hard to port and ease off on the mainsail, and—"

Blake did things his own way and quickly got the *Argos* headed straight for the cap. Just as Mr. Schenley was straining down with his arm stretched out to grab the cap as they went past, it began to sink. The brass ornament on the front of it twinkled once as it went under, and then Mr. Schenley's reaching fingers closed—on water.

"Blankety-blank!" yelled the pudgy man, pounding his fist on the bow.

They all looked back to where the cap had slowly sunk beneath the waves, and Julia giggled again. She put her hand over her mouth right away and tried to make her face straight again.

"Gee, I guess you just weren't supposed to get your cap back, Mr. Schenley," she said.

He glared over his shoulder at her.

"When I want to hear from you I'll tell you," he snapped. "Young man, sail this boat into the harbor. I've had enough of this tub."

"Yes, sir!" said Blake promptly.

Mr. Schenley squirmed back off the foredeck and scrunched down on the seat across from the girls. He stuffed tobacco into his big pipe, used up four matches trying to light it, and finally got it going. His face had settled into a dull red color and his jaw was still stuck out like a bulldog's. For a while he sat puffing out fierce clouds of smoke and scowling into the distance. Nobody spoke.

After a while the man turned and saw the little smile on Blake's face. Mr. Schenley showed his big crooked teeth in a sneer.

"Don't get the idea I'm not going to buy this boat now, because I am," he growled. "My mind is made up more than ever."

If he had wanted to make Blake stop smiling that hopeful way, he had succeeded. It was plain that Blake had been hoping Mr. Schenley would change his mind because of having so much trouble with the *Argos*.

"There's nothing basically wrong with this boat," Mr. Schenley went on. "What she needs is to be rigged properly and she'll handle all right."

Blake stared as though he had not heard him right.

"Gee, Mr. Schenley, you wouldn't *rig* her differently, would you? Why, she's perfect the way she is. She wouldn't look right—"

"I'll decide that," snapped the man. He pulled out his handkerchief and wiped spray off his bald head. "You just tend to getting her back to her mooring now."

When they were back in the harbor, Blake tied up the *Argos* at her mooring and lowered her sails and put everything in order. They all climbed into the dory and Blake rowed toward shore. Mr. Schenley was impatient to get there.

"All right, all right, put your back into it. Where did you learn to row?" he demanded, though Blake was rowing them along at a pretty good speed, considering the amount of weight there was in the boat. Then, as they got near shore, Mr. Schenley remembered he was barefooted.

"Oh . . . !" He ground his teeth together to keep

from swearing. "I left my shoes and socks in that fool sailboat!"

"Do you want me to go back, sir?"

"No, I've had enough of your rowing. I'll get there my-self." Quite plainly, he had had enough of their company, too. "Just get me ashore."

By this time they were almost there, but Mr. Schenley was so impatient that he swung his feet over the side and stepped into the water before the boat had quite touched the shore.

He must have thought he was stepping into shallow water, but instead of stopping at the ankles he went right on in up to his waist. Even his blue coat with the brass buttons got wet.

"I forgot to tell you, there's a deep hole on that side, Mr. Schenley," said Blake.

"I know there's a hole, you idiot! I'm standing in it!"

bellowed Mr. Schenley. His face was almost purple, and he shook a finger at Blake. "You think you're funny, don't you? Well, don't ever come around begging for a ride in the *Argos* when she's mine, because you won't get it, see? Now get going before I lose my temper and give you the hiding you deserve!" he yelled, and turned to flounder onto shore.

Blake turned the boat around and started rowing away as fast as he could. Mr. Schenley was so mad he was not watching where he was going. There were a lot of stones on the bottom and it was easy to stumble. All at once there was a big splash, and when they looked back all they could see of Mr. Schenley was his arms and legs thrashing around.

When he did regain his feet he stamped up onto the shore without glancing around again. To make matters worse, Julia had giggled one of her silly giggles, and now, as Mr. Schenley disappeared around a corner of the boat shop, they could not control themselves.

"Oh, golly!" said Blake, holding his sides. "Okay, Julia, you wanted to row back, so come on, change places with me. I can't row any more."

"All right, I'll try," said Julia, but when she tried she began to laugh so hard that *she* couldn't row either. They just floated around for a while until she could stop enough to start rowing, and that took a long time.

CHAPTER 7

Secrets of the Sand

"BLAKE," said Aunt Sally next morning, "you march right back up to your room and put on your sneakers. You, too, Julia."

"Aw, Mom!"

"You're not to climb around on that old wreck in your bare feet. It must be full of splinters and rusty nails. I'm glad to see Susie has sense enough to wear *her* sneakers."

Susie's were blue and white, and brand new. To tell the truth, she had not even been thinking about the wreck when she put them on. She was thinking about all the things that might be on the beach, things she did not want to step on. She looked down at the sneakers and wiggled her toes in them, glad to have their protection.

The cousins were all wearing their bathing suits, in case they wanted to go for a swim. Susie could not swim, but she thought that maybe she would want to wade around a little in shallow water, close to shore.

"We'll come down around noontime and bring a picnic lunch," Aunt Sally told them.

As they wheeled out their bicycles Blake cupped his hands around his mouth and called up the road.

"Billy!"

"Will he have Caroline with him, Julia?"

"Heavens, no, Susie. Not when he's going to be working around."

They heard a screen door slam and the scrape of a bike rest being kicked up; and then Billy turned into the road, looking like a round dumpling perched on his under-sized two-wheeler.

He was carrying a shovel crosswise in front of him, holding onto shovel and handlebars at the same time. He looked like one of those performers in a circus who use a long bar to help balance themselves on a tightrope.

"Oh, I forgot my shovel," said Blake as soon as he saw Billy, and ran back to the barn. He came out carrying one like Billy's, but he carried it on his shoulder and steered his bike with one hand and sometimes no hands.

They pedaled up the road that ran to the beach. Tina came running along behind them with her tail wagging and her pink tongue lolling out of her mouth and her plump body moving in a waddly way.

It was bright and sunny, and warmer than usual for an early June day on Cape Cod. The flowers in the yards nodded gaily as they passed, but Susie was not happy. She was worrying about the sharks and crabs and jelly-fish that might be in the water where they were going.

"Shall we take our secret trail?" Julia asked as they rode along.

"Sure. It'll save time," said Blake.

"What secret trail?" asked Susie.

They told her about it. It was an old gravel path through the woods that used to go back to a summer cottage. The cottage had burned down long ago. Weeds and trees had grown up all around it, but it was still all right for bicycles.

"It goes almost all the way through the woods, and then we leave our bikes at the edge of the woods. It's a lot closer to our shipwreck than going straight down to the beach," Blake explained.

Billy was riding on ahead, and none of them could very well pass him because of the way his shovel stuck out on both sides. Now he started pedaling as hard as his short, fat legs would go. He looked back over his shoulder at the others with a cocky grin.

"Bet I beat you all!"

He had such a head start that there was no chance to catch up with him, so the three cousins did not try. But

Billy kept at it and soon looked back at them once more.

"I win!" he cried, as he swerved off the road onto the path.

However, he had been so busy thinking about getting there first that he forgot about how narrow the path was. His long shovel smacked against a small tree on each side of the path.

"Oof!" grunted Billy. His bicycle kept on going, right out from under him. One instant Billy was hanging in mid-air like a balloon; the next, he was flat on his back in the path, still holding onto his shovel.

He scrambled quickly to his feet and struggled to get his breath. He looked at Susie.

"Bet you can't do that," he panted, trying to pretend that he had meant to do it.

"Who are you trying to fool?" scoffed Blake, as Billy went to get his bike. It had gone off the path to one side. "You didn't mean to do that."

"I did so."

"You did not. You'd better let *me* lead the way," said Blake, putting his shovel back on his shoulder again and pushing off down the path on his bicycle. "Anybody who doesn't know any better than to carry a shovel that way—"

Crack!

Blake had forgotten about the low branches that hung

over the path. His shovel hit against one of them, and he lost his balance and tumbled off into the bushes. That made Julia and Susie laugh so hard that their bicycles began to wobble around, and they both ran off the path, too. Susie fell off and landed on some soft pine needles. She was not hurt a bit; but, as she landed, something moved close by her, making the pine needles rustle.

"Oh!" Susie screamed in terror and jumped to her feet, looking over her shoulder in time to see a flash of white tail bob out of sight.

"What's the matter with her?" jeered Billy Snow. "Even scared of a rabbit."

Susie felt foolish. She glared at Billy. "I didn't know *what* it was."

Blake got to his feet and picked up his shovel. "Well, I guess we'd better walk our bikes the rest of the way. It'll be easier."

"I couldn't ride anyway," said Julia. "My stomach hurts too much from laughing."

They went on through the woods along the path to where a part of a fire-blackened chimney still stood.

"That's where the cottage was," said Julia.

From the back of the clearing another path that was not graveled ran on through the woods. They took that. In a minute or two they came out of the woods and were on the edge of the sand dunes.

The sand dunes were hills of sand, with a few bushes and some beach grass growing on them. Beyond the dunes was the beach. Far out across the sand was the water.

"What a long way you have to walk to go swimming here," said Susie. "I thought the water would be much closer than that."

"Silly, it's low tide now," snorted Blake. "Those are the flats. When it's high tide the water comes in and covers them up."

"Gee, who doesn't know that," said Billy.

"You're so smart, I guess you know everything," retorted Susie, with a toss of her head. "Everything except how to carry a shovel on a bicycle, anyway," she added.

"That's right," said Blake, laughing. "Okay, let's leave our bikes here."

They walked up and down across the dunes; and when they were down in the sandy valleys between the dunes they could no longer see the beach or the water, but only the sky.

Finally they crossed the ridge of dunes and reached the beach. It was wide and smooth, and it slanted a little bit downhill to the flats, which seemed smooth and almost perfectly level.

"Now we have to walk to eastward about half a mile, and then we'll be there," said Blake.

"My, it's a long way, isn't it?" said Susie.

"Good thing. Too many people would come snooping around," said Billy. "We're trying to keep it a secret."

"A secret? You told the conductor on the train about it," Susie reminded him. Billy looked guilty and scowled at her.

"Well, he won't come over to see, and besides he didn't believe me anyway," he said quickly, but Blake bawled him out for telling.

"As it is, we've got to work fast and find out if there's any treasure in her before the summer people start coming on vacation," grumbled Blake. "When *they* all get here they'll find out about our ship and they'll come to gawk at it and pull it to pieces."

"Maybe they won't walk this far," said Susie.

"Some will," said Julia gloomily, and they all started to walk a little faster.

After a while they came to a point of the beach that stuck out into the water. The point was covered with rocks and some big boulders. They were not like rocks on a hill, because their edges were all worn smooth by the waves, and many of them were round. A high bluff ran along the back of the beach there.

"It's just around this point, now."

They played follow-the-leader across the rocks, jumping from one to another. Then they walked around the side of the biggest boulder, and there ahead was the shipwreck.

They were right—her timbers did look like the ribs of some prehistoric monster sticking out of the sand. The ribs stuck up higher than Blake's head, and there were a lot of them. The wreck was lying sideways against the bluff, where it had been completely covered by the sand of the beach until the storm had uncovered it.

Enough of the back end was showing so that even Susie, who did not know much about boats, could tell that it had been one. All around it were signs of where the boys had shoveled away sand, but it looked as if an awful lot of sand was left to be shoveled. Not even half of the boat was uncovered yet.

"Oh, I'm excited! Maybe she's full of treasure!" cried Julia. "Let's start digging right away. I want to dig some."

"*We'll* do the digging, Billy and me," growled Blake. "We want to get this job done."

"Blake, do you really think this is the boat you were talking about?"

"You mean the *Island Gull*, Susie? Sure I do. Dad looked it up in the old registry at the courthouse. It was sixty-two feet long and had two masts. This must have been about that long, and the mast we found is too near the stern to be the only mast. If there were three, it would be the mizzenmast."

"The what?"

"The mizzenmast. That's the rear mast on a three-master."

"Oh." Susie did not have any idea what he was talking about, but she nodded solemnly. It was wonderful, all the things Blake seemed to know.

"Come on, let's climb up and go aboard her and I'll show you," said Blake.

"Going aboard" the boat was easily done by climbing up the side of the bluff. Almost all her deck boards were gone, but she was so full of sand that it was almost like a deck.

"This here was the quarter-deck," said Blake, striding about like a ship captain. "On some ships, like galleons, it was called the poop-deck. That's spelled p-o-o-p, but you pronounce it 'pope.' Billy, let's get busy and dig out some more of the stern."

Blake and Billy climbed down and went to work with their shovels. Tina did some digging, too, in between running in circles around the boulders. She always acted silly when she came to the beach.

Julia ran down to the edge of the beach and looked around until she found a couple of large, smooth shells shaped like the bowl of a spoon. She gave one to Susie.

"Here, we can use these shells to scoop sand with."

"What kind of shell is this?" It was as big as both her hands. It was white and shiny on the inside, and chalky white on the outside.

"That's half of a sea-clam shell. Come on, let's go aboard again and we can scoop out sand up there."

They climbed back up on the deck and started scooping sand and throwing it over the side. For a while Julia worked as fast as she could and made the sand fly. The boys were making the sand fly with their shovels, too. It was a hot day, though, and soon they began to slow down. Every time Billy dug a shovelful of sand they could all hear him puff.

"Whew!" said Blake, stopping to mop his face with his

bandana handkerchief. "This is going to be a long job. Julia, you can use the shovel for a while now."

Julia looked down at Blake and the shovel and seemed to have lost her eagerness.

"I'll use it pretty soon."

"Huh! Just like a girl. Talks about wanting to use your shovel, and then when you let her she doesn't want to."

"I will pretty soon. I'm tired now. I've been working up here."

Blake sat down and stared around him at the tons of sand that filled the old wreck .

"Golly, this is an awful big job—but if only we can find some kind of treasure in her it'll be worth it."

"We'll find hundreds of bars of gold and give them to ol' Mr. Cartwright for the *Argos*, and then will we have fun!" crowed Billy Snow.

"Man, oh, man," said Blake, his eyes sparkling as he imagined what it would be like. It made him so excited that he got up and dug like fury again for several minutes, and so did Billy, until they were too tired to lift their shovels any more. Blake's shoulders slumped again, and he shook his head.

"Gee, we dig and dig and don't seem to get anywhere," he muttered. He mopped his face with his arm and looked out at the water. "Well, come on, let's knock off and go for a swim."

CHAPTER 8

Susie Sneakers

THEY ALL sat down on the sand and took off their sneakers. Susie took hers off, too, because they were full of sand. She shook it out and then put them back on again.

"What are you putting your sneakers back on for?" asked Billy. "We're going out on the flats."

Susie looked up. None of the others were putting their sneakers back on.

"Well, I'm certainly not going to walk out there in my bare feet."

"Well, for gosh sakes, why not?"

"Well, I'm just not. I don't want to."

"You're a scairdy-cat. Got to wear your sneakers," cried Billy. " Susie Sneakers, that's what we ought to call you."

"Susie Sneakers. That's right," laughed Blake.

"You're Susie Sneakers, you're Susie Sneakers!" chanted Billy, dancing around in front of her and pointing.

Susie stuck her tongue out at him.

"I don't care!" she said, but her face grew red and she wished they would stop making fun of her. And she knew one thing—she *hated* Billy Snow.

"What are you worried about, Susie? Nothing's going to hurt you," said Julia, but they could not talk Susie out of wearing her sneakers. The boys kept on making fun of her for being a sissy, until Julia finally helped her out a little.

"Well, gee whiz, let her get used to things first," she said. "She doesn't know anything about beaches. Soon as she knows, she won't mind going barefoot."

Along the edge of the shore was a shelf of black, earthy, rubbery stuff that was very slippery.

"Watch your step. This is sedge and it's skiddy," said Blake. He was carrying his shovel, and when they had crossed the sedge and were on wet sand with little rivulets of water running through it he stopped.

"Hey, look, Susie."

They all gathered around where he was pointing.

"See that little hole?"

She had to look closely, because it was a round hole in the sand no bigger around than a pencil lead.

"What is it?"

"Sea-worm hole. Let's take a look at him. We'll be wanting some before long for fishing."

Blake dug up a shovelful of sand and dumped it to one side. "There he is. A good one, too," he said. Susie jumped back and squealed.

A huge red and green worm as long as Caroline, with what looked like hundreds of legs, was wiggling around on the sand.

"Is *that* a sea worm?"

"Yep," said Billy, and picked it up. "They have pinchers, too, and they can—Ow!"

All at once he dropped the worm and rubbed his finger.

"I was going to say they can pinch."

The worm had dropped right back into the hole Blake had dug. The hole was already filling up with water. The sea worm swam down through the water, stuck its head in the sand, and began to disappear.

"Watch him go," said Blake. "That's why you have to grab them quick sometimes when you're digging them."

"How did that hole get full of water?"

"Oh, out here on the flats there is water under all the sand, not very far down. Anywhere you dig you hit water."

They walked out across the flats, and Susie noticed that they were not completely level after all. The sand was higher in some places than others and here and there they had to wade through little streams of water. Susie watched her step very carefully; but, except for a few small snails, she saw no living thing on the clean brown sand.

The sun was so bright that she had to squint a little. In every direction now, whichever way she looked, they were surrounded by vast flat spaces; and the blue sky seemed higher and broader and rounder than she had ever seen it before.

Far ahead of them, little waves lapped at the edge of the sand, and beyond was the great blue-green expanse of water. Far out were a couple of black specks on the water which Blake said were boats. In the distance everything was a little hazy, and it was hard to see exactly where the water ended and the sky began.

Birds were flying back and forth along the flats, or walking on the sand. Blake said they were seagulls and sandpipers and plovers. He pointed to one little bird that was running along quickly from one shell to another, flipping up each one with its long, sharp bill. The little bird was brisk and businesslike, and paused only long enough to give one keen glance under each shell.

"That's a turnstone."

"A turn-shell, it should be called."

"He turns stones over the same way. He's looking to see if a crab or anything else good to eat is hiding under them."

After a while the sand sloped down and they had to wade through water up to their knees before the sand sloped up again and out of the water.

"Now we're getting to the outer bars," said Blake. He looked behind them at the shore, as he had done several times before. "When you're out like this on the flats you want to always keep checking to make sure the sea isn't coming in behind you. When the tide turns it can come in pretty fast sometimes, and you don't want to be caught out here when it does. Not much danger of that today. Not much wind, and the tides aren't running high."

"Friday's sea-clamming tide," Billy said. "My pa's going out."

"Do you know what a sea-clamming tide is, Susie?"

asked Julia, and hurried on without waiting for her to answer. "Well, it's a real low tide. We only get them once a month, because when the high tides are highest the low tides are lowest."

"I'll explain about tides when we get home," said Blake. "I'll show you on the tide table. Well, here's the last bar. This is as far as we can go—except that we can still wade out quite a way without getting into deep water. But I don't want to catch any of you kids going too far," Blake added in his best grown-up voice, "because the tide will be turning soon and we'll have to start back. Dad said I was to be in charge of things when we were on the beach."

"Not of me, you ain't in charge," said Billy impudently, and ran off into the water.

"If I have to come after you I'll duck you good."

"Let's all take a swim," cried Julia, and she ran straight into the water. "Ooh—it's cold! But it's good! Last one in is a monkey!"

"That'll be Susie Sneakers," said Billy. He was floating around on his back, squirting mouthfuls of water up into the air.

Susie hesitated and looked at the water. It looked nice, but what about all the things that might be in it? Standing at the water's edge, she found it was so clear that she could see the bottom, all clean sand rippled into long rolls like a washboard. She waded in cautiously. The water felt good on her feet, but when it touched her knees it began to feel cold.

Blake came galloping by and grabbed her arm. He pulled her in with him.

"Stop it! Stob-b-bubb-glubb—" Susie's mouth filled with water. She thrashed around, trying to get her feet down. "I can't swim!" she managed to gurgle.

Her feet touched bottom. She stood up and found that the water hardly reached her waist. Coughing and sputtering, Susie looked around at Blake angrily.

"Darn you, Blake!"

"Well, that's the way to get in—all at once. Then the water doesn't feel cold any more."

Susie realized that she had forgotten all about the water, and as Blake said, it did not feel so cold now. She could still see the bottom all around her blue sneakers, too.

Billy swam past, doing an overhand stroke with his face under water. He stopped and stood up.

"Hey, you still have your sneakers on!" he jeered at Susie. She tossed her head.

"Well, what of it? Why shouldn't I?"

"Only sissies wear sneakers in swimming."

"You can step on seaweed and jellyfish if you want to, but I'm not going to," she said hotly. "My mother says jellyfish can sting you."

"Aw, shucks!" said Billy disgustedly. "Maybe they can,

but they never stung me. Anyway, there aren't any jelly-fish around here today."

"Billy's right," said Julia. "But gee, Susie, you really mean you don't know how to swim?"

"Yes."

"Can't you even float?"

"No."

"Oh, but that's easy, especially in salt water."

"Sure," said Blake. "Salt water is very buoyant. That means it holds you up. All you have to do is lie back on it and you'll float. Come on, try it."

"No! I don't trust Billy."

"I won't let him try any tricks, and I'll hold you up. Hold your breath and do a dead man's float on your face. That's easiest of all."

By coaxing her Blake finally got Susie to try a dead man's float. When she tried it, she found it really was easy. After she got used to that she tried it on her back.

"Now kick your feet and you'll travel through the water," said Blake.

Susie kicked her feet and found she was moving forward.

"See? Before you know it you'll be swimming!"

"You could kick better with your sneakers off," said Julia, and it was true that they felt heavy.

Susie practiced floating for quite a while and began to

enjoy it more and more. She tried a dead man's float again, and this time she even opened her eyes under water.

She could see every inch of the bottom very clearly, and there was nothing down there but clean rippled sand and a few small rocks. She wondered if she dared take her sneakers off for a few minutes while she was in the water. That would show Billy Snow a thing or two.

In another instant Susie might have had enough courage to march out of the water and take her sneakers off— for a minute or two. Just then, however, directly under her nose, something beside one of those rocks suddenly moved. It scuttled sideways away from the rock. It was green and had claws. Susie retreated hastily.

"Oh! There's a big crab! Watch out!" she cried. "There! And you said I shouldn't wear sneakers!"

"Aw, who's afraid of an old crab?" scoffed Billy. "Susie Sneakers, that's who."

"He's more afraid of you than you are of him," said Blake. "See how he's burying himself in the sand?"

"He'll nip your toe sometimes if you get it too near, but it really doesn't hurt much," said Julia. "It just surprises you."

"That sounds like a terrible surprise to *me*," snapped Susie.

It was true that the crab was not exactly attacking them. It had backed itself into the sand on the bottom, digging with its back legs, until it was all covered up except for the pincers of its big claw. All it seemed to want to do was escape and hide.

"Shucks, I'll *let* him nip my toe, and see if I care!" said Billy.

"You wouldn't!"

"Who wouldn't?" He put his foot in front of the crab's claw and touched it with his big toe. Quick as a wink, it gave his toe a good pinch and held on.

"Ow!" Billy jerked his foot up, and the crab let go. It went swimming swiftly away again to the bottom.

"Oh, my goodness! Did he bite it off? Is it bleeding?" cried Susie, grabbing Billy's leg as he swung it up. "Let me see!"

"Hey, let go!" said Billy, and tumbled over backward with a splash. He rolled around, spitting out water, and glared at Susie. "Gosh darn it, you're worse'n a crab!"

"I was only worried about your old toe!"

"Heck, it's all right. It didn't hurt hardly at all."

"Is it bleeding?"

"Of course not." This time Billy held onto Blake and lifted his leg out of the water to prove that his toe was all right. As soon as he held his foot up, Blake gave him a shove and down went Billy again with another big splash.

They wrestled around in the water, having fun, but Susie was no longer enjoying herself. She was wading as fast as she could into shallower water and keeping a sharp lookout for crabs as she went. Presently Blake said it was time to start back, so they got out and began the long walk to shore.

"The tide's turned. It's coming in now. See how the waves sweep around the end of this bar and break on the back side exactly the same way they do on the front side? Dad showed me that once. He said that's why if you were out here in a storm or a fog it might be hard to tell which way to walk if you got mixed up. Another thing, you couldn't tell if you were going the right way by whether or not the water got shallower, because sometimes it's deeper on the back side of a bar than on the front side— like right here on this one."

It was true. Instead of being shallow near the back edge of the bar and gradually getting deeper, the way it did off the front edge, the water was up to their waists before they had taken more than two or three steps.

"Gee, it was fun to take a swim," said Julia. "Mommy says the water is still too cold for her, but I don't think it's bad at all. Didn't you like it, Susie?"

Susie hesitated.

"Well . . . I'd like it better if I didn't have to keep watching for things."

"But you don't have to. There's nothing that's really going to hurt you."

They were all looking at Susie now, and she felt ashamed. She knew they thought she was a sissy, but she couldn't help it. She wished miserably that she were home and had never come to Cape Cod in the first place. And then Billy Snow made matters worse by being a smart-aleck again.

"Well, I can tell you one thing, I wouldn't wear sneakers in swimming if the whole bottom was covered with crabs." He danced around her and began to point at her. "Susie Sne-e-e-eakers, Susie-e-e Sne-e-eakers!"

CHAPTER **9**

Susie Does a Puzzle

"Gee, tomorrow is Dad's birthday," said Blake as they walked back to the shore. "Wait'll you see the present I have for him."

"How does it look with what I got you in Providence?" asked Billy slyly.

"Swell!"

"What did you get for Blake in Providence?"

"Never you mind, Julia."

"What *is* your present, Blake?"

"You'll find out."

"I'll tell you what I've got for Daddy if you'll tell me what you've got."

"I already know what you've got."

"Oh, you're just being mean!"

"Listen, you're such a blabbermouth you might let it slip out if I told you. I'm not taking any chances."

79

Julia begged and wheedled, but Blake would not tell her.

"I've got a present for Uncle Gurney in my trunk," said Susie. "My mother put it in and told me to be sure and remember."

"Swell. Well, let's start digging some more around our wreck," said Blake. "We've got to shovel away enough sand to find out if there's anything left of the cabin. That's where the treasure will most likely be, if there is any."

"Pretty soon Mommy and Daddy should be coming down with the lunch. Anyway, I hope so. I'm getting awful hungry."

They all talked about how hungry they were, and all at once Susie felt as if she were going to starve if she did not get some food soon.

"Do people always get so hungry here?"

"Sure. The sea air gives you an appetite."

"Give me your shovel, Blake. I want to do some digging."

"You can have it pretty soon, Julia, after I dig awhile."

"Oh, darn! When I want to dig, you won't let me."

"In a minute, in a minute!" snapped Blake, beginning to dig very energetically.

"Let me use your shovel, then, Billy."

"In a minute," said Billy, beginning to dig, too.

Julia and Susie climbed up on deck and went back to

their clam shells. Julia had some more things to say about
the boys, and when she started scooping sand some of it
"accidentally" fell on Blake's head.

For a while they all dug, and then Blake stopped and
stood back away from the stern of the wreck.

"Hey! Come here, everybody, and look at this!"

Billy dropped his shovel and the girls jumped down.

"Look! When you get the sun on the stern just right,
you can see some letters on it!"

Only part of the stern was left. Some of it had been
smashed. On the boards that were still in place, however,
it was as Blake had said. When you stood so that the
light hit the stern boards exactly right, you could faintly
see the outlines of four letters. They were very dim, but
Billy and Julia and Susie could see them, too. They had
to take turns standing exactly where Blake had been standing.

"S-L-A-N— the *Slan!*" said Blake. "The letters are
right in the center of the stern, so that must be the whole
name."

"The *Slan*. What a funny name," said Julia. "I don't
think it's a very pretty name, either. If I had a boat I would
never name it the *Slan*."

"Gee, and I was *sure* it was the *Island Gull*. Now we'll
have to see if we can find somebody who's heard of a boat
called the *Slan*."

Susie still stood and studied the letters intently. Picking up a stick, she drew them in the sand—SLAN—and studied them some more. She had often played word games with her mother and father, and she was pretty good at them.

An idea buzzed into her mind.

"Blake! Look what happens when you put a letter on

each side of those," she said excitedly, and drew two more letters in the sand, one on each side:

ISLAND

"Golly!" cried Blake.

"Jumpin' juniper!" said Billy. "Susie Sneakers is right. Island! *Island Gull!*"

Blake was down on his hands and knees, squinting at the stern from all different angles.

"If that was *Island*, then *Gull* ought to be under it in the center, in the same size letters— Yes. I can see what could be a G and a U. I can't see any L's, but I can see a G and a U."

He pointed them out, and they all looked. Though the G and U were even fainter, there was not much question about them.

"What's going on here?" asked a deep voice, and they all jumped.

They looked up, and there was Uncle Gurney grinning down at them. He was carrying a picnic basket. Aunt Sally appeared beside him.

"Dad! Hey, Dad—Mom—come look at what we discovered," cried Blake. They made Uncle Gurney and Aunt Sally hurry down and stand in the place where they could see the letters.

"You see? S-L-A-N. Don't tell them, anybody. Isn't

that a funny name? I'll bet you'll never guess—well, I mean—"

Blake did not quite know what to say to make them guess, without giving anything away. Susie noticed the letters she had drawn in the sand. She edged over and rubbed them out with her foot.

"Hey! Who's kicking sand in my shoes?" asked her uncle.

"I'm sorry, Uncle Gurney, I thought I saw an awful-looking bug."

"Oh. Well, let's see, now. The *Slan*. H'm. What an odd name," he said, rubbing his chin and rolling his eyes around. "I've never heard of such an odd name, have you, Sally?"

"I certainly haven't. What do you suppose it means?"

"I'll bet it's some kind of bird. Come to think of it, isn't there a rosy-breasted slan that lives on the coast of Greenland and eats goofer nuts?"

"Aw, you've guessed! I can tell when you're fooling, 'cause you always start saying silly things," said Julia, giving her father a push.

"Susie figured it out," said Blake.

"I've played word games a lot with Mommy and Daddy," Susie explained.

"You were pretty smart to work it out, though, Susie," said Aunt Sally.

"Sure you were. I'm an old word-game player myself, and you can't fool us experts," said Uncle Gurney. "I'll bet your aunt hasn't figured it out yet, though."

"Oh, is that so? You're not the only smarty in the family. I'll show you," said Aunt Sally.

She picked up a stick and drew the letters I S L A N D on the sand—exactly where Susie had drawn hers.

They all let out a howl at once.

"So! You saw those letters in the sand, eh?" said Uncle Gurney accusingly.

"Ha! If *you* know they were there, then *you* saw them too!" said Aunt Sally, and then the laugh was on Uncle Gurney. "So I guess Susie is the only one who really worked it out for herself, after all. Well, who's ready to eat?"

"Oh, boy!"

Nobody had to be asked twice. For the next few minutes they ate sandwiches and drank fruit drinks as fast as Aunt Sally would hand them out.

"All right, now, slow down. Here's another half a sandwich for each of you, and the first one who finishes his— doesn't get any more."

They all tried to eat more slowly then, but even so before they knew it they were each down to a crust. They began acting silly.

"Look, this is how they eat in society. Little bitty bites," said Billy, and he started nibbling his crust with his front teeth, a crumb at a time.

"Aunt Sally, what if nobody gets through first? Can we all have another sandwich then?"

"Why, yes, Susie, but I don't see how you're going to work it for nobody to get through first."

"Everybody put your crust in your mouth at once," cried Susie. "Ready? One—two—three—go!"

Four crusts were popped in at the same instant. Aunt Sally laughed and hugged Susie.

"That's pretty good!"

"I think that deserves more sandwiches all around," said Uncle Gurney, handing each of them another half. "Susie, you're getting sharp as a tack. It must be this good Cape Cod air. Who wants more fruit drink?"

Susie watched Uncle Gurney fill the four cups they instantly held out to him. She ate her sandwich, and she felt warm and good inside from having such nice things said about her. Then Billy Snow had to spoil it all, as usual.

"Susie won't take off her sneakers to go in the water. She's scared she'll get a little nip from an ol' crab or something."

Susie's toes scringed inside her blue sneakers at the thought of being nipped, and she made a face at Billy. She felt Uncle Gurney's and Aunt Sally's eyes on her, and hung her head.

"Well, Susie has to get used to things here first," said Aunt Sally, but Susie knew she was just being kind about it. She wished she could take off her sneakers and run around barefooted like the others, but she knew she would never, never, be able to do that.

Uncle Gurney must have known how she felt, and how embarrassed she was, because he started talking about something else.

"Blake, when I went to the post office this morning to get the mail, several people asked me about what went on between you and Mr. Schenley yesterday. Are you sure you told it to us exactly the way it happened?"

"Yes, sir."

"You weren't fresh to Mr. Schenley?"

"No, sir. We didn't even laugh, except once or twice when we couldn't help it, did we, Susie?"

"Oh, no, Uncle Gurney."

"Silly Julia, she always has to giggle," growled Blake, looking at his sister.

"Well, who wouldn't giggle? He looked so funny, flopping around in the water," said Julia, and they burst out laughing all over again. The night before, when they had told the story at supper, Uncle Gurney and Aunt Sally had tried not to laugh; but before they had finished the grown-ups had been laughing as hard as the children. In fact, Uncle Gurney had all but fallen out of his chair.

Uncle Gurney coughed now and tried to pull his face straight again.

"We shouldn't laugh, because I'm a bit worried about this. Mr. Schenley was hopping mad about the whole thing, and from what I hear he's going around telling people he'll see to it that you won't get to work at the boat shop, Blake."

"What?" Blake jumped to his feet, and his face was pale. "He can't make Mr. McGill not let me work, can he?"

Uncle Gurney looked troubled, but he shook his head slowly.

"No, I don't think so, but I wouldn't be too sure. But at any rate, try not to have any more trouble with Mr. Schenley. I want to see you have that sailboat if we can possibly work it out, and getting that man mad won't help things any. I don't know exactly what he could do, but he might think of something."

CHAPTER 10

Susie Meets Stuffy

AFTER LUNCH Uncle Gurney helped with what he called the "excavations." He took a shovel and dug some more sand away from the stern, and he also worked up on deck.

The *Island Gull* looked as if its whole front end was stuck into the sandbank at an angle, but Uncle Gurney did not think that was actually the case.

"I'm afraid we won't find the whole boat here. As a matter of fact, I think most of what we'll find is already in plain sight. When the *Island Gull* was wrecked, the waves probably beat her to pieces. Part of the stern broke off and stayed together, and this is it. There may be pieces of the boat scattered all over the place, but I don't think you'll find another section of any size."

"Aw, shucks." Blake leaned on his shovel and looked at the wreck, disappointed. "I was hoping the whole ship was here. But still, the stern end is more likely to be the part with the treasure in it."

"I wouldn't count on getting rich, Blake," said Uncle Gurney. "I'm afraid the *Island Gull* came along too late to go out and capture any Spanish galleons full of gold and silver."

"I don't care about that, Dad. All I want is just enough gold or silver to buy the *Argos*."

"Well, I hope you find it. But you can't do all the digging at once, and I think you've done enough for one day."

"Well, I could dig some more, but I'm worried about my job," said Blake. "I'm going over to the boat shop and ask Mr. McGill about it."

"Maybe you'd better."

They walked back across the dunes to where the bicycles were. From there the children rode on ahead while the grown-ups walked up the path to the car.

"Can we go with you, Blake?" asked Julia.

"I guess so."

They crossed the harbor with Blake at the oars, looking concerned and thoughtful as he planned what he would say to Mr. McGill. Each stroke of the oars was clean and sure as he rowed, so that even Susie could not help but feel how smoothly the boat moved along. And that old Mr. Schenley had pretended he wasn't good!

When they entered the shop Mr. McGill was painting the bottom of a boat with copper-colored paint. He
looked around, coughed gruffly, and turned back to his
work.

"Hello, Mr. McGill," said Blake in a small voice.

"H'm," said Mr. McGill. His tone was not very en-
couraging.

Blake fidgeted for a minute. They waited, and Susie
was glad she was not the one who had to think of what
to say next.

"That was a terrible thing that happened to Mr.
Schenley the other day," Blake said finally. "I was awful
sorry."

The wiry little man snorted and rolled his eyes up at
Blake.

"I'll bet you were," he said. "I suppose that's why we could hear you all laughing clear up here."

"Gee, Mr. McGill, we couldn't help it," said Blake.

"It was my fault," said Julia. "I started giggling."

The small man straightened up with a great snapping of joints and swung around slowly, looking them over, while they held their breath.

"H'm. Well, Mr. Schenley has been after me not to hire you, and I can't say as I blame him too much." Mr. McGill watched their faces fall, and his squinting eyes and his straight mouth did not change. "But at the same time I've got to give you a chance. So you've still got your job."

"Oh, boy! Thanks, Mr. McGill!" yelled Blake, and he let out a whoop that made the poor man back up a step.

"Cut that out, you'll bust my eardrums!" He tapped Blake's shoulder. "Now you remember, young fellow, you'd better be nice to Mr. Schenley and not cross him, or you'll be in trouble. Understand?"

"Sure, Mr. McGill! Don't worry about me."

"All right then. I'll expect you Saturday."

"Yes, sir."

They ran out of the shop as if someone were chasing them. Blake was so happy he even let Julia row them back across the harbor.

When they were home again, Blake told his parents

what Mr. McGill had said. Uncle Gurney said Mr. Mc-
Gill was being eminently fair.

Then they went outside and Blake said, "Billy, let's go
up to your house and see Caroline."

"Aw, Susie Sneakers is scared," jeered Billy.

"No, I'm not!" Actually, she wished Blake had not
suggested going to visit a snake, small or otherwise, but
she did not like to admit it. She could not truly relax
when Caroline was around, no matter what Uncle Gurney said about her fine personality.

"All right, let's go," said Billy, and they ran up the
road to his house, which was a rambling old Cape Cod
cottage. Billy led the way to a shed in the rear.

"Billy's mother won't let him keep Caroline in the
house, so he has to keep her out here," Julia explained.

"I'm going to make her a regular cage with a glass
front, first chance I get."

"I'm going to help him," said Blake. "After all, Billy,
you helped me with you-know-what. My birthday present for Dad."

"What is your present?" demanded Julia. "I wish you
wouldn't be so mysterious."

"Never mind. Tomorrow morning you'll know."

Inside the shed was a workbench. On one end of it
stood a wooden box with a hole in the top covered with
wire screen. Billy opened the box and looked in.

"Hi, Caroline," he said, and lifted her out. Caroline wrapped her tail around his little finger and curled up in his palm. She looked up at him, and anyone could see it was a devoted glance.

"See how she wraps her tail around his finger?" asked Julia. "That's so she won't fall."

"Nice Caroline," said Billy, stroking her head with one finger.

He was amazingly gentle with her, for a boy who was so rough and rowdy in other ways. Sitting there quietly in his hand, Caroline looked quite small and not so terrifying to Susie any more, though she would have hated to touch her.

"Aren't they awful to touch?" she asked Julia.

"I should say not. Caroline is nice and warm and dry, and—why, she's just like velvet," said Julia. "Here, let me have her for a minute, Billy."

"Okay, but be careful." Billy tipped Caroline into Julia's hands and carefully unwrapped her tail from his finger. Caroline did not seem to mind, but she immediately wrapped it around Julia's finger.

"See? That's one thing she's learned to do," said Billy proudly.

They took her outside on the lawn and let her nose around in the grass for a while, while they sat down around her in a circle. Susie sat a little farther away than the others, and she scooted back hastily once when Caroline turned her way.

"Shucks, don't be scared. Put your hand down and she'll come and sit right in it."

"No, thank you!"

After a while Billy put Caroline back in her box, and they went outside and played catch until Aunt Sally called them home and gave them jobs to do before supper.

Susie finished her chores first and came back to the kitchen. Uncle Gurney was there, too, talking to Aunt Sally. Susie sat down on a stool.

"We were playing with Caroline this afternoon," she told them.

"Oh? Did you make friends with her?" asked Uncle Gurney.

"Well, I didn't hold her, or anything like that, but I watched her."

Aunt Sally, who had been hunting through a drawer, straightened up and said, "Oh, now I remember where that recipe is I'm looking for. It's in a box in the attic."

Uncle Gurney groaned.

"I suppose I'm elected to go get it. I don't suppose I happen to have a niece in this whole wide world who would—"

"May I get it for you?" asked Susie.

"Well, now, that's real nice of you to save your poor old uncle's bones a trip all the way up to the attic. Where's the recipe you want, Sally?"

"On the right hand side of the attic as you go up the steps there's a closet, and in the closet is a little chest of drawers. In the second drawer there's a white box. Bring me the box, dear."

"Got it? Right hand side—closet—little chest—white box," said Uncle Gurney. "The light switch is beside the door to your left as you start up the steps."

Susie went upstairs and found the door to the attic and the light switch all right, but when she flipped the switch nothing happened. She flipped it off and on again, but still nothing happened.

Feeble rays of late afternoon light were filtering through the small attic window, but even so the attic looked gloomy as she peered up the stairs. Shadows rushed away into corners to collect there blackly, and the air was close and still.

Susie started to call down and tell her uncle the light was out, but stopped as she heard her cousins come into the kitchen. They would think she was afraid.

Susie turned and walked up the steps into the gloomy attic. Her legs felt as stiff as a doll's and the backs of them tingled, but she kept going. It would only take a few seconds to go to the closet and get the box, and she

could hurry right downstairs again. *Then* she could tell
Uncle Gurney the light was not working, and they would
all know she had not been scared.

Several pieces of furniture had been turned into ghosts
by the white dust covers that were draped over them, and
bulky clothes-bags were hanging in one shadowy corner
near the door of the closet. Susie marched boldly past
them with her eyes straight ahead.

"I'm not going to start imagining things. There's not
a thing up here but old furniture and clothes-bags," she
said, and she even whistled a dry little whistle to show
she was not afraid. Of course, it was kind of creepy to
open a closet door in a gloomy attic; but, after all, what
could be in it but a little chest of drawers?

Susie pulled open the door—and there on the closet
shelf, looking down at her with fierce eyes, stood a huge
owl.

For a second Susie could not move. Then she let out a scream and slammed the door shut. She ran down the attic stairs and on down to the living room. She almost ran right into Uncle Gurney, who was hurrying to see what was the matter.

"There's an owl in the closet!" Susie cried. "A great big owl!"

"An owl? Are you sure?" Uncle Gurney was bewildered. "How could an owl get in that closet?"

Blake jumped up and began stamping around.

"Oh, darn you, Susie!" he yelled. "What were you doing in that closet?"

"I sent her up," explained Aunt Sally. "And what do you know about this affair, young man?"

Blake looked very annoyed.

"All I know is she's spoiled my surprise birthday present for Dad, and I've been working on it for weeks and weeks—that's all," he declared, shooting dark glances at Susie.

"You mean your present is an *owl?*"

"Yes."

"A live one?"

"Of course not," snorted Blake. "A stuffed one. I stuffed him myself. Wally Williams showed me how. Billy Snow made a special trip to a store when he was in Providence and got some special glass eyes for me, because Wally didn't have the right kind for owls. And now Susie had to spoil it all. Gosh!"

"Now, just a minute," said Aunt Sally, putting her arm around Susie, whose lip was beginning to tremble. "It was *not* Susie's fault. I sent her up to the attic, and I told her to look in the closet for a box of clippings I wanted. It was my fault if it was anybody's, though why you chose that place to hide an owl is more than I can see."

"Well, who'd think anybody would look in there?" grumbled Blake. "It *would* have to be right now. Why did you have to send her up right now, darn it, Mom?"

"Now, hold on. No use crying over spilled milk, or spilled beans, either," began Uncle Gurney.

"That's right, Susie spilled the beans," said Julia, laughing and clapping her hands. "Oh, Daddy, you're so silly!" she said, and they all laughed, except Blake. He started to laugh, but then remembered that he was still angry.

"Well, anyway, children, I don't see that it will hurt for me to get one present a little ahead of time. I *feel* a year older already even though I won't be until tomorrow, so why not? Go get my present and let's see it."

"Then I want to give you my present, too."

"No, Julia, only Blake gets to give his present tonight, to make up for spoiling his surprise."

Blake brightened up considerably, while Julia complained that he always got to do everything and she never got to do anything. He went tearing upstairs to get his present. In a minute they heard him coming down again.

"All right, now, everybody sit down and get ready for the big entrance," said Uncle Gurney, quickly taking the chairs from the kitchen table and lining them up. "It isn't every day in the week that somebody gives me a stuffed owl."

They all sat down and waited expectantly. Blake walked into the kitchen carefully carrying his present in front of him. Everybody burst out with cries of admiration.

"Ooh!"

"Magnificent!"

"Why, it looks as if it could fly away any minute!"

"I think the owl deserves a nice hand," said Uncle Gurney, and they clapped their hands as hard as they could. "Take a bow, Blake."

Blake bowed and presented the owl to his father. Blake had a silly grin on his face and looked very proud.

"He isn't perfect, but Wally said he was good for a first try. I had trouble making him stand up exactly right, and I don't think I stuffed his chest quite enough."

"Why, he's a splendid bird," said Uncle Gurney, turning the owl around and examining it from all sides. "We must give him a name. I'll tell you what—let's call him Stuffy. Stuffy, the Stuffed Owl."

"Stuffy. That's good," Julia nodded thoughtfully.

"Okay, we'll call him Stuffy," agreed Blake.

"Well, I certainly don't blame Susie for being scared when she saw him in the closet," said Aunt Sally. "You know, that was really quite a compliment, Blake. It shows how lifelike he looks."

"Yes, I guess that's so," said Blake, and looked at Susie with a grin, to show he was not mad at her any more. "Scared you, huh?"

"Well, it would have scared you, too, if you hadn't known about it," said Susie.

"I still didn't get my box of clippings, what with all the excitement," said Aunt Sally.

"I'll go get it," said Susie, jumping up. "I'm not scared now!"

CHAPTER **11**

More Trouble with Mr. Schenley

"THE BAY's full of mackerel!"

It was Blake who came bursting in with the news. Uncle Gurney, who was enjoying a second cup of coffee and smoking his new pipe, asked, "Who says so?"

"Billy's father. Can you go out, Dad?"

Aunt Sally was gathering up the wrappings from Uncle Gurney's birthday presents. Uncle Gurney made a great ceremony of unwrapping them, and they all felt good because he was so pleased.

"Well, I don't know," he said now. "After the big time I've just had I don't know whether I could stand much more excitement."

"Mr. Snow's getting ready to go out. He says Billy and I can come along—but I'd rather go with you, Dad."

"No, Blake, you go with them and I'll take the girls." Uncle Gurney turned to Susie, who was helping dry the breakfast dishes. "Want to go mackerel fishing, Susie?"

"Oh, yes. And you can use your new fish knife."

"I sure can, Susie."

"Oh, darn. I wish you could wear *my* present," said Julia.

"Well, Julia, I think a chef's apron with funny sayings written all over it is a grand thing to wear when I'm cooking a steak in the back yard, but hardly the thing for the bay—unless, of course, we're going to broil our mackerel right in the boat."

"I'd sure hate to see you try that, Dad!" said Blake.

"Don't feel bad, though, Julia." Uncle Gurney held out his pipe. "I can't take your mother's present along either. A new pipe has to be broken in very carefully. It mustn't be smoked out of doors at first, especially not in a boat with the wind blowing."

Susie had a question.

"Do we have to put those big sea worms on our hooks?"

Blake snorted.

"Shucks, no. You just use a little spinner."

"What's that?"

"Bring your tackle box and show her, Blake."

"Okay, Dad, and my glass rod. I've got a glass rod that's swell for mackerel fishing, Susie. Wait'll you see."

Blake rushed down into the basement and returned with his equipment. His rod was light and short and was made of flexible glass. He opened his tackle box and took out a gadget that had three small fishhooks on the end. The three hooks were on one shaft. Some red and white feathers and a thin, shiny piece of metal dangled from the shaft. The metal spun around when Blake flicked it with his finger.

"See? That's the spinner. These three hooks are called a gang hook. This is what you use to catch mackerel. You don't have to use any bait. They think the red and white feathers are something good to eat."

Susie was glad to hear that sea worms were not going to come along on their fishing trip. She watched the preparations with interest.

Uncle Gurney collected his fishing equipment, Aunt Sally packed a lunch for them, and they piled into the station wagon—all except Blake, that is. He ran up the road to ride with Billy and his father in their truck.

"I want to ride in the back of the truck, too, Daddy," Julia said.

"You keep me company going down, and maybe you can ride in it coming home."

For the fishing trip they brought along the outboard

motor in the back of the station wagon. Mr. Snow had a boat and motor similar to Uncle Gurney's. When they had loaded the boats and the motors were in place, they started down the channel.

"Bet we catch more mackerel than you do," Uncle Gurney called.

"Bet you don't," yelled both boys.

"Well, we'll see."

"Susie-e Sne-e-eakers! Don't get your sneakers wet!" called Billy Snow, and Susie stuck her tongue out at him. She hated that name.

The water was calm and sparkling. The only real waves were the ones the boat made as it ploughed through the water. The sun was shining in an enormous bowl of blue sky with a fringe of fleecy white clouds floating along near the horizon. The air smelled tangy and bracing, and it filled Susie with the special exhilaration of the sea. It was exciting to be in a boat going out on Cape Cod Bay for the first time in her life.

Other boats were already going back and forth, some distance offshore. They were traveling along side by side, back and forth. They would go in one direction for a long way, then turn and come back. The biggest boat with the biggest motor went past as they neared the fishing grounds, and Susie thought that the man running the boat looked familiar.

"Julia, isn't that man in the big boat Mr. Schenley?"
Julia looked and made a face.

"Yes. Wouldn't he have to be out here!"

"Now, Julia, I don't want any freshness out of you," said Uncle Gurney. "Just don't pay any attention to him."

"Don't worry, Daddy, I won't," sniffed Julia, turning up her nose.

Mr. Schenley was wearing a cap with a long, long bill, like fishermen wear, and his eyes were concealed by sunglasses. Great puffs of smoke were coming from his bulldog pipe. His line was never idle as he trolled it along behind his boat in the water. His rod flicked incessantly as he gave his line a series of impatient jerks. It was as if he were signaling a message to the mackerel —"Come, come! These other people may have lots of time, but I'm a busy and important man, so kindly start striking my hook!"

Uncle Gurney slowed their boat to trolling speed. He gave Susie a glass rod and showed her how to work the reel. She let her line out, watched it trail through the water, and practiced reeling it in and letting it out. Julia had her line in, too; and so did the boys in Mr. Snow's boat, putt-putting along beside them, twenty yards off their starboard side.

Susie looked around at the boys, afraid that any mo-

ment one of them would catch a fish before she or
Julia did. While she was looking, Mr. Schenley went
past again in his big boat, still sending the mackerel his
irritable messages.

"I wonder if Mr. Schenley has caught any yet, Uncle
Gurney?"

"I don't think so. Nobody seems to have taken any
fish so far."

"Hurry, Julia. Try and be first," Susie cried. "Don't let
the boys—"

Her rod jerked hard and wiggled, and the wiggle sent
a thrill tingling up her spine and right down to her very
toes.

"Julia! Uncle Gurney!" she cried. "I—I— What do I
do now?"

"Susie's got a mackerel!" cried Julia. "Don't lose him,
Susie!"

"Start reeling him in, Susie. Steady, now. Don't get
excited," said Uncle Gurney, who sounded pretty excited himself. "Don't let him have any slack, keep your
line taut, and keep reeling."

Susie reeled as fast as she could, and she could feel the
mackerel pulling her line. Her heart felt as if it were going to pop right out of her, as she kept thinking, "Oh,
I mustn't lose my fish. I mustn't lose it."

It seemed as if she had to reel and reel forever, and all

the time she was afraid the tugging would stop and the fish would escape.

The boat was dancing along and little waves were rolling out from behind the motor. Spray was flying in the air. Finally she saw the knot of the loop in her line come into sight, and a few feet behind it she saw a splash and a dark blue flash as the mackerel came to the top of the water for a split second.

"There he is! Bring him in!"

She reeled harder than ever. The fish came alongside swiftly now.

"All right, swing him into the boat."

Susie pulled up on her rod, and there was the mackerel, dangling in the air above the water. She swung her rod toward the boat, and Uncle Gurney made a grab for her line. He missed. The mackerel smacked him squarely in the face.

"Oh, I'm sorry!" cried Susie, and pulled her rod back. The swinging fish slapped against her cheek. For an instant it was off the hook, free in mid-air. Then it dropped into the bottom of the boat and started flopping over the floorboards from stem to stern.

"Grab him, Julia."

Julia seized the fish by the tail and held on. "Here, Daddy."

"Okay, I've got him." He held the shiny mackerel

high in the air, pointed to Susie, and called to the other boat. "First fish!"

"Beginner's luck," they roared back.

Uncle Gurney pulled the fish box out from under the center thwart and threw the mackerel in.

"Nice work, Susie. Where's your hook?"

Susie looked. One of the barbs was hooked through her dungarees, and it was only by good luck that it had not hooked her, too.

"Oh, my gosh. That was a close one. That's my fault," said her uncle. "I should have given you a little drill. You've always got to be careful with your hook when you're fishing. When you get a fish in the boat, put down your rod so's your line will be slack and the hook will stay in the bottom of the boat on the floorboards. Even then you want to keep track of it. Can you get the hook loose?"

Susie managed to work the barb carefully through the cloth. It was hard to do, particularly since her hands were trembling. She could hear her fish's tail slapping the bottom of the fish box—her fish. Her first fish.

"I've got it out," she said, holding up the hook.

"Daddy! I've got a strike! I've got a fish, too!" cried Julia, starting to reel in as fast as she could.

"Fine. Stay with him. Susie, get your line back over the side. Hurry! When the fish are biting you have to work fast."

Susie soon had another fish. This time she got him in the boat without hitting her uncle in the face. Julia already had her fish in, and she was taking him off the hook. Susie was so eager to catch more fish that she took her second one off the hook by herself. The mackerel were trim, blue-black fish about a foot long and were so beautiful she did not mind handling them. She put her line over the side again.

Uncle Gurney was watching her, and he looked pleased. "Susie, I think you've found something you like."

"I love it, Uncle Gurney."

They went along for a minute without any more strikes —they called it a "strike" when a fish grabbed the hook.

"Reel in your lines, girls, and we'll make a quick turn," said Uncle Gurney. "We seem to have run through the school. You know, most fish swim around together in groups of their own kind, Susie. We call those groups a school of fish."

"They go to school to learn how to bite our fishhooks," said Julia. "Okay, Daddy, I'm reeled in close. Are you, Susie?"

"Yes, my spinner is in the water beside the boat," said Susie, leaning over and looking down at it.

"That's fine. Leave it there," said Uncle Gurney. "The reason you have to reel in when we're going to make a sharp turn is that your lines might get tangled up if you didn't. Also, they would sink to the bottom as we turned and might get caught in the weeds or rocks."

As they reversed their direction they saw that both the boys were reeling hard. Billy's eyes were popping, his head was nodding with every turn of the reel, and his chubby cheeks were shaking. All at once he swung his fish up out of the water and yelled proudly. With a flip it came off the hook and splashed back in the water.

"Billy lost his fish," cried Julia. "Look at him shake his fist."

Billy got his line back in the water immediately, though, as a real fisherman should, and when the boats passed he already had another mackerel on his hook.

In the meantime, Mr. Schenley always seemed to be in the wrong place. Almost everybody else in the other boats was catching mackerel, but he had yet to land his first. His pipe was going like a smokestack and his big teeth looked ready to bite its stem in two.

"Your friend doesn't seem to be having much luck," said Uncle Gurney. He meant Mr. Schenley, and of course he was only joking when he called him their friend.

"Well, I hope he doesn't get a single one," said Julia.

"What a mean little girl. Poor Mr. Schenley."

"Well, I don't care, Daddy."

"I'll tell you one thing, he won't get any unless he changes his style. He's going too fast. But never mind that—I don't want to hear any fresh talk about him from you, Julia."

"Oh, all right, Daddy."

"He's probably a perfectly nice man, once you get to know him. He doesn't really appear to be such a terrible— Why, that big jerk!" Uncle Gurney's tone changed completely. "Look at him cut across everybody's lines!"

"Who?"

"That idiot Schenley!" snapped Uncle Gurney, forgetting what he had been saying. "When there's a number of boats out like this each boat should stay in its own lane. He's liable to get somebody's line hooked onto his, or get one fouled in his propeller—"

All at once Blake's reel sang out with such a whir that they all heard it. That meant that something was pulling on his line very hard. Mr. Snow stopped his motor at once, and Uncle Gurney stopped, too.

"Hey!" Mr. Snow waved his arms, and Mr. Schenley, who was a short distance away, also cut his motor.

"I knew it. A line's fouled in Schenley's propeller— and wouldn't it have to be Blake's?" groaned Uncle Gurney.

"What happened?" asked Susie, who did not understand.

"Well, Mr. Schenley's propeller caught Blake's line and the line began to wrap around the shaft of the propeller. Now it's tangled up."

When Mr. Schenley tipped his big outboard motor up out of the water Susie saw the propeller. Using a pair of pliers, he removed the pin from the propeller and took it off the shaft. He had to do that to free the line. When he realized whose line it was he seemed to swell up all over as he glared across the water with his eyes nearly popping out of their pouches. He pointed at Blake.

"You again! How many times are you going to get in my hair?"

"What hair?" whispered Julia. "He hasn't got any."

"That will be enough of that, Julia," Uncle Gurney whispered sternly. Susie tried not to giggle.

"You shouldn't cut across other people's lines like that, mister," said Mr. Snow in a mild, quiet voice. He started up his motor again before Mr. Schenley could reply. Uncle Gurney started his motor, too, and as he did Susie saw a splash near the end of Mr. Schenley's boat and heard him let out a terrible yell.

"What happened?" she asked her uncle. He had turned away and seemed to be choking, as though he were trying not to laugh.

"Children, I'm terribly afraid poor Mr. Schenley just managed to drop his propeller overboard."

Uncle Gurney was right. Mr. Schenley had to be towed back to the harbor by another boat. The rest of them caught more mackerel, and when they finally stopped and went in they had so many fish that they took some to four of their neighbors.

Home again after the fish were taken care of, Blake washed out their fish box with a hose and set it in the sun to dry.

"I hope Mr. Schenley won't try to take it out on you because of what happened out there, Blake," said Uncle Gurney, while they were standing outside in the yard.

"Gee, I hope not, Dad," said Blake.

"It was his own fault, every bit of it, but that doesn't always make a difference to his kind." Uncle Gurney stared into space, frowning for a minute. He patted Blake's shoulder. "Well, let's cross that bridge when we come to it—if we do."

Uncle Gurney went inside. Blake sat down on the back steps and looked uneasy.

"Aw, stop worrying, Blake," said Billy. "Everybody that was out there saw it was his own fault."

"Sure, it was," said Julia.

"Tell you what—come on over to my house and help me get started on that new cage for Caroline."

Blake sighed and got slowly to his feet, trying to shake off his worry. "Well . . . Okay, let's go."

"What can we do to help?" asked Julia. That brought back some of Blake's spirit.

"Oh, I've got a swell job for you and Susie."

"What, Blake?"

"You can lean against the shed and hold it up."

"Aw, you're worse than Daddy. You're always fooling."

They walked over to Billy's and went into the shed. Billy took Caroline's box down off the workbench.

"Let's say hello to Caroline. How are you today, Caroline?"

He opened the top of the box and looked in.

"Caroline?" He put his hand in. "Come on, Caroline." Then he felt around. "Caroline!" Billy's voice squeaked in an anxious way. He tipped the box toward the light.

"What's the matter, Billy? Where is she?"

Billy peered into every corner of the box. His round face was as white as the sails of the *Argos*.

"She's gone!"

CHAPTER 12

Needle in a Haystack

"I just don't see how she could have got out unless somebody let her out—or stole her," said Billy Snow. Tears were rolling down his plump cheeks. He sniffled noisily.

Julia was weeping, too.

"Poor Caroline," she moaned.

"Well, I don't know," muttered Blake. He was examining the box carefully, looking over every inch of it, particularly the screen top. He lifted one corner of it. "Hey! See here? It's loose at this corner."

"Oh, but golly, such a little bit," said Susie. "Caroline could never squeeze through there."

"Oh, you don't think so, huh? You don't know," said Blake. "Why, snakes can get through the littlest cracks you ever saw. They can flatten their heads out and stretch their bodies, and—gee, Caroline could make that easy, couldn't she, Billy?"

Billy was examining the screen with a long face—long for him, anyway.

"Gee, I expect so. I'll bet that's where she got out, all right. If only we'd got going on her new cage a little bit sooner." Billy wiped his eyes and nose with the back of his arm and sniffled again. "Well, come on, let's start looking for her. Look everywhere. Maybe she's still in here somewhere. Look under everything and around everything—and be careful. Don't knock anything over, it might fall on her and hurt her."

They began carefully looking over and around and under and between everything in the shed. Even Susie helped search, though she did not know whether to be afraid she might see Caroline or afraid she might not.

In one dusty corner she came across an old flowerpot. It had not been disturbed for a long time. A big spider web ran from the corner to the flowerpot. The pot was turned upside down, and like all clay flowerpots it had a round hole in the bottom. The hole was certainly plenty big enough for Caroline. Susie tipped the pot over.

"Yi!"

She let out a yell as a huge brown spider scuttled out and ran away along the edge of the wall.

"Find her?" cried Billy quickly.

"No, a spider."

"Oh, heck."

Susie turned the pot back upside down and looked under three more. There was nothing under any of them, not even spiders.

None of the others was having any better luck.

"Well, I guess she isn't in here," Billy said finally in a gloomy voice. "I guess we'd better start looking around outside and hope she hasn't gone very far."

They felt badly discouraged. There were so many places Caroline might be, and so much trouble she might get into. It was like looking for a needle in a haystack. In fact, it was worse. At least a needle didn't roam around.

"Gee, Caroline has the whole great outdoors to be in now," said Blake. "She could be anywhere. Well, anyway, let's keep on looking."

They searched around the outside of the shed and every inch of the yard until Aunt Sally called the cousins home to supper. They left Billy and trudged home to announce the bad news.

"That's terrible! Poor Caroline," said Uncle Gurney.

"That's just like a woman, though—she had to get curious. Because she found a little loose place in the screen, she felt she had to crawl through it and see what was going on outside."

"Do you think she might come back, Daddy?"

Uncle Gurney shook his head. "I'm afraid not. I don't think snakes are much like homing pigeons."

"I'm sorry for Billy," said Aunt Sally. "He must feel awful."

"He sure does, Mom."

"It's a funny thing about that boy. He certainly has a touch with animals," said Uncle Gurney. "They all seem to trust him."

"Then why did Caroline run away?" asked Julia.

"I told you. She was curious. It's the nature of the beast, as the expression goes. It doesn't mean she wasn't happy with Billy. And I'll bet you that wherever she is right now, she wishes she were snug in her cage again."

Susie gulped as she listened. Poor Caroline. And poor Billy. She had wished the most awful things about Billy when he pulled tricks on her; but now, when she thought of the misery in his round face, she felt sorry for him and wished very much that somehow they could find Caroline. It was hard to understand, the way you could hate somebody when he was teasing you and then feel so sorry when something bad happened to him. One thing was sure— she would never have wished anything as bad as *this* even on Billy Snow.

Dessert was special that night—ice cream and birthday cake. While Uncle Gurney was cutting his cake, Julia remembered something he had promised them at breakfast. After supper they would have a game of cards to celebrate his birthday.

When they had finished supper, Aunt Sally said, "All right, let's clear up the table and wash the dishes so we can play a game."

With so many helpers she had more dish-dryers than she needed, so she gave Susie a special job.

"Susie, will you take that recipe box back to the attic and put it away for me? Gurney, did you put a new bulb in the attic light?"

"Yes, it's all right now."

"Do you mind, Susie?"

"I should say not, Aunt Sally."

As she picked up the box and started upstairs, Susie heard Billy Snow knock on the back door and come in. Aunt Sally tried to cheer him up with ice cream and cake, but he said, "No, thanks." His voice sounded small and sad, instead of firm and loud the way it usually was.

Susie hurried upstairs to the attic door and snapped on the light. It worked this time. The attic was bright as she went up. Even so, she was startled for a moment by what she saw on top of the bureau. Then she laughed.

"Stuffy!" she said, looking at the owl. "My goodness, Blake will be mad if he finds out that Uncle Gurney has already brought you up here."

She put the box in the closet and descended the steps again, thinking how odd it was that Uncle Gurney would do a thing like that. She was surprised at him. It was kind of mean, when Blake had worked so hard on Stuffy and was so proud of him. Uncle Gurney had made such a fuss over Stuffy, too, and had said he was going to keep him on the desk in his study.

She decided she wouldn't say anything about it, so that Blake's feelings wouldn't be hurt. But still . . . How could Blake miss seeing that Stuffy was gone? She went to the door of Uncle Gurney's study and looked in to see if you could notice at once that the owl was missing.

Susie blinked.

Stuffy *was* there. He was sitting right on the desk where he was supposed to be.

"Stuffy!" Susie's eyes grew almost as round as his. "How did you get down here?"

For a moment she was almost afraid to go near him, but then she decided that was silly. A stuffed bird! She edged into the room and walked very slowly toward him. As she came closer she relaxed. There was the wooden stand he stood on. She reached out and touched him, and of course he did not move, because he was a stuffed owl and nothing more.

But if that was so . . .

What was that owl doing up in the attic?

Susie smiled. Of course! Blake must have secretly stuffed *another* owl, and now he was going to surprise his mother with that one.

Susie glanced at Stuffy and frowned. She felt a little worried. Stuffy was nice and all that, but at the same time how many stuffed owls would Aunt Sally and Uncle Gurney want to have around the house? Wasn't one about enough?

She thought this over for a minute and decided to sneak back and have another look at the one in the attic. Maybe it was a different kind of owl that Blake had stuffed this time. Maybe it was special, or a rare species.

Susie returned to the attic. She stopped halfway up the steps and stared thoughtfully at the owl. It seemed to stare back.

"Gee, you almost look as if you could be alive," she said.

The owl's eyes slowly closed and opened again.

Susie gasped. "Oh, my goodness!"

She ducked her head and raced for the kitchen.

"Uncle Gurney! There's an owl in the attic! A live owl!"

Uncle Gurney did not believe her, of course. He chuckled and glanced at Aunt Sally.

"All right, what's the idea of putting my friend Stuffy in the attic? I'm surprised at you, Mother—I didn't think you objected to letting him hold down papers on my desk."

Aunt Sally shook her head; but before she could speak, Susie burst out again.

"No, Uncle Gurney, this isn't Stuffy. Stuffy is still on your desk. This is *another* owl."

Of course then they all thought of the same thing she had thought of. Billy Snow spoke first.

"Did you stuff another owl, Blake?"

Blake shook his head. "I sure didn't!"

"And besides, this owl *blinked* at me," added Susie.

That settled it. They started upstairs. Uncle Gurney went first, followed by Blake and Billy, and the women-folk were allowed to bring up the rear. On his way to the second floor Uncle Gurney stopped and they all bumped together like a line of cars.

"Oops! Excuse me," he said, catching his balance. "I just thought of something. Let's not rush into this thing without a plan of action. Remember your Boy Scout motto, boys—'Be Prepared.' Julia, you're at the end of the line—run down to the basement and fetch one of the crab nets."

"All right, but wait for me." Julia went flying, while her mother called out the usual warning to be careful on those basement stairs. Julia's feet beat a tattoo up and down the steps, and in no time she was back with a crab net.

The net was attached to a loop of wire on a long wooden handle. They passed it up the stairs to Uncle Gurney.

"All right, now. Onward and upward," he said, pointing ahead with the crab net. "And not too much noise. Let's not get our feathered friend upset. You ladies let us men go up first. If it looks safe for you to come and watch we'll tell you."

Julia complained loudly at this suggestion and was sternly shushed for making so much noise. Uncle Gurney and the boys crept up the steep steps on tiptoe and fingertips. From the top they motioned to Aunt Sally and the girls.

"All right, come on up far enough to see. He's sitting there quietly."

"He must be sick," said Billy. "He'd act more excited and fly around if he wasn't."

"I think you're right," said Uncle Gurney. "He doesn't *look* well, now that you mention it. He looks humped-up and unhappy, even for an owl."

"How did he get in here?" asked Aunt Sally. "Did that screen come off the window again?"

They glanced down at the other end of the attic, where the window was. The screen was lying flat on the floor.

"Now, listen to me," Aunt Sally told Uncle Gurney, "that screen has got to be fixed properly. I can't have flies and wasps and owls and heaven knows what else roosting in my attic."

"We'll fix it right away, won't we, Blake? Well, now, I'd better net our friend here."

"Mr. Winthrop, I'll bet I can pick him up and hold him without any net," said Billy. "The net'll only bother him."

Uncle Gurney looked down at the boy thoughtfully.

"Well, as I've said before, you've got a touch with animals and birds, Billy. I guess if you want to try it's all right, but be careful. An owl can give you a good bite with that curved beak of his, and his claws can be mean, too."

"I'll be careful. Old owl won't hurt me, will you?" Billy said to the owl, and walked very slowly toward it, watching every move it made. It did not move except to edge back and forth.

As Billy came close it raised its wings feebly, opened its mouth and let out a weak hiss, but it did not fly at him. Billy's hands seemed not to move very fast, and yet all at once he was holding the owl around the back of the neck with one hand and around the legs with the other.

He held it firmly and yet so gently that it did not struggle. There was no question about it, either—the owl did not feel well enough to struggle.

"Nice work, Billy," said Uncle Gurney. "Let's take him downstairs."

They clattered downstairs to the kitchen and stood in a circle around Billy, looking at the owl.

"What we need right now is a good owl doctor," said Uncle Gurney. "How in the world do you go about prescribing medicine for a sick owl?"

Billy was looking the owl over carefully. It seemed to sense that it did not have to be afraid of him, because it was quiet and scarcely moved. Billy touched its head. The owl shook it as though something hurt.

"Here. Look here," said Billy. Very carefully he lifted some of the feathers on its head. Under them was an ugly cut. "See? He hit his head hard against something and cut it."

"By George, you're right. Maybe he's dazed, more than anything," said Uncle Gurney, inspecting the cut.

"I can help him if that's it," said Billy. "I can put some medicine on it."

"You mean iodine?" cried Julia, horrified.

"Heck, no. My ma's got some new stuff that's a salve and won't sting him."

"Will you bandage his head?"

"No, he'd only claw off a bandage."

"You can lock him in the shed overnight and then we can see how he is in the morning."

"But what if Caroline should come back?"

"Gee, that's right."

"Why, what's the matter with that?" asked Susie. "Caroline wouldn't hurt him, would she?"

They all laughed, and Uncle Gurney gave her a pat on the shoulder.

"No—but he might hurt Caroline, Susie. An owl would probably consider Caroline a delicious meal."

"Oh! Gee! Well, what are you going to do, Billy?"

"Why don't you put him in Caroline's old cage? It's plenty big enough for him," said Blake.

"Sure, we can put a piece of a branch in for him to stand on. Come on, let's go do it."

"And be sure to lock the cage up, so that Caroline won't come home and find an unpleasant surprise for her," Uncle Gurney called after them.

They went over to Billy's and watched while he put salve on the owl's cut. They fixed up Caroline's old cage and put the owl in it.

"We're going to play cards, Billy," said Blake when they had finished. "Want to come over and play?"

Billy shook his head gloomily.

"No, I got things to do."

When they came home, Uncle Gurney said, "Well, maybe the owl will make up a little for losing poor Caroline." But Blake shook his head.

"I don't think anything could take Caroline's place, Dad."

It seemed as if Blake were right, too, because after they had finished playing cards and it was time to go to bed, somebody happened to glance out the window.

"Look, over on the Snows' lawn."

Across the road and through the trees they could see a circle of light slowly moving around on the ground. Billy was still searching for Caroline by the light of a flashlight.

"Poor Billy," murmured Aunt Sally. "Poor little fellow."

CHAPTER **13**

The Fight

IN THE morning there were chores to be done. Susie and
Julia dried the breakfast dishes and dusted the living-
room furniture (which Julia said she hated to do worse
than anything). Blake emptied the garbage and all the
wastebaskets. When he had finished he trundled the
power mower up the street to mow a neighbor's lawn.

After a while Julia managed to disappear in the direction of the Snows' house, to help Billy search for his
missing pet. Susie and her aunt finished hanging out the
wash and were coming in through the basement door
when they heard the telephone ringing upstairs. Susie
raced ahead to answer.

It was Mr. McGill. He gave her his message in a gruff
voice and hung up.

"Mr. McGill wants to see Blake," Susie reported to
Aunt Sally.

"I suppose Mr. Schenley—" began Aunt Sally, but stopped and set her mouth in a firm line. "Well, I want to go to the post office, so I'll drive by and tell Blake. Would you like to ride with me?"

"Yes, Aunt Sally. I have a letter to mail to Mommy, and maybe there will be a letter for me."

Blake only nodded when his mother told him Mr. McGill had phoned. He said he would go to the boat shop as soon as he had finished the lawn.

"I'll tell him exactly what happened, and when he hears I was out with Mr. Snow he'll know I wasn't doing anything wrong, because Mr. Snow wouldn't allow it. Everybody knows he's one of the best fishermen around."

At the post office a letter from her mother was waiting for Susie. She tore it open eagerly and read it aloud to her aunt as they rode home. Near the end her mother said she hoped Susie was not feeling too homesick and was sure that after she became more accustomed to such different surroundings she would be all right.

"For a girl who's only been here a few days I think you're doing pretty well," said Aunt Sally. "I was a tiny bit worried about you at first, but I haven't seen any long faces lately. Have you been homesick, Susie?"

"Well, yes, I was at first," Susie admitted, "and I think I still would feel homesick, only that right now I'm so busy worrying about Blake and the *Argos*, and

Billy and Caroline, that I don't seem to have a minute for anything else."

Aunt Sally's eyes twinkled, and she gave Susie a warm hug with one arm as they drove along.

"You keep on doing that. We'd all be happier if we spent more time worrying about other people's problems and less about our own. Now I'll tell you what—when we get home I wonder if you'll take the flower scissors and cut a nice bouquet for the table?"

Aunt Sally knew that would please Susie, because she loved flowers so much. As soon as they reached home Susie took the scissors and went out to the side yard. She spent a long time choosing which flowers to cut; and when she brought them into the house, Blake was turning into the drive on his bike.

"I stopped and went down to see Mr. McGill," he told Aunt Sally and Susie. "Everything was like I said. When I told Mr. McGill I was out in Mr. Josh Snow's boat, that was enough. The only thing he said was that he hoped I'd stay clear of Mr. Schenley from now on, so he wouldn't keep trying to make trouble for me."

"Well, I hope you do, too," said Aunt Sally. "Just stay away from him."

"I will. Well, I want to check the tires on my bike, and then I'll go back and finish that lawn," said Blake, and went into the barn.

Susie and her aunt arranged the flowers in a vase, and Aunt Sally stood back to study the effect.

"I think we really need about three more marigolds right here to make it perfect."

"I'll get them," said Susie, and hurried outside.

As she circled the bushes that fringed the side yard she saw a dark-haired boy on a bicycle stop in the road and wheel his bike over to peer intently at something in the grass. He was larger than Blake, and older. His bicycle was a new and fancy one and seemed to have everything on it in the way of a spotlight or horn or basket or tool kit or taillight that anybody could possibly invent.

When he saw Susie coming he held up his hand and hissed, "Stop!" in a loud whisper. He glared at her so fiercely that she actually did stop in her tracks.

She craned her neck to see what he was watching and noticed a strange cat crouched in the shadow of a big spruce tree. It was hunched down and twitching its tail the way a cat does when it is about to pounce.

And then she saw what the cat was about to pounce on. Not two feet away, motionless beside a clump of dried grass, was a green grass snake.

There was no time to stop and think things over. Susie acted without thinking.

"Scat!" she shouted. She darted forward and snatched up the small snake before the cat could recover from its surprise. Tina came running around the corner, barking excitedly as she caught the scent of the cat, and Pussy streaked across the street and up a tree.

"Hey, what's the idea!" The boy dumped his bicycle on the road and came toward her looking mean and angry. "I wanted to see the cat grab that snake."

"Blake!" cried Susie as loudly as she could. "Blake, come here!"

"I saw that snake first, so give it here," said the dark-haired boy roughly.

"No!"

"I want to put him in a jar of alcohol and keep him."

"You can't do that! I think it's Caroline!"

"Caroline? What are you talking about?" sneered the boy. "Let me have it."

Susie turned and ran. The boy would have caught her if at that instant Blake hadn't come running around the corner of the house. Billy and Julia followed.

"You leave my cousin alone!" cried Blake, running squarely into the strange boy and giving him a push that sent him head over heels backward on the grass.

He scrambled to his feet with his fists clenched.

"Why, you—I'll teach you a lesson!" he gritted, and smashed Blake in the mouth. Blake's fist pounded back at him, left and right, landing solidly on his face. The larger boy staggered back, and his nose began to bleed.

"I'll beat you good for that!" he warned, and dived
for Blake to wrestle him to the ground. They went down
in a tangle of arms and legs and rolled over and over,
fists flying, muscles straining, Blake wriggled out of a
hold and sprang to his feet with his fists ready.

The other boy came at him swinging wildly. Blake
crouched down in a boxer's stance. He remembered to
punch. Every time the larger boy swung Blake ducked
under his swing and then stepped in and slammed hard
jabs to his face and body.

In a rage the boy kicked at Blake. His foot lashed out
and barely missed Blake. Now it was Blake's turn to be
furious. He put his head down and began smashing the
boy with a flurry of punches that drove him back, looking frightened and beaten.

"I'll teach you to kick at *me!*" said Blake, jamming a hard right into his ribs. The boy stumbled backward and toppled into a little hollow filled with a tangle of dead tree limbs. Uncle Gurney had been intending to chop up that wood ever since the last hurricane had blown it down, but it was still there. Blake's opponent flapped around like a duck trying to get loose and climb to his feet. When he finally did pull himself up there was a ripping sound. A worried look appeared on his face. He reached for the seat of his pants.

"Darn you, I'll get you for this!" he shouted, backing away from them to his bicycle. He was almost crying, he was so angry. He picked up his bicycle and jumped on quickly, but not before they saw that the seat of his pants had a big, big rip in it. He began pedaling as fast as he could and was halfway down the road before they began to laugh.

"Golly, that was a swell fight! That was better than television," said Billy. "You sure took care of that creep."

Blake wiped the blood off his mouth.

"He was a pain in the neck. Who was he, anyway?"

"I don't know. I never saw him before."

"Neither have I. Must be some new summer kid. Why was he bothering you, anyway, Susie?"

"Oh!" That made Susie remember what the excitement had made her forget. She remembered she was holding a green grass snake in her hand, and she didn't even know for sure it was Caroline.

At first she almost let go, but it was very quiet in her hand. It was also warm and dry, not cold and slimy the way she had thought it would be. She looked at it, and noticed something that made her shout with excitement.

"Oh, Billy! Look!"

She held up her hand and pointed to the little snake's tail. It was wrapped around her finger.

Billy stared at it for an instant and his eyes grew round as two moons. He let out a yell of pure joy.

"Caroline!"

He held out his hands. Caroline crawled into them and wrapped her tail around one of his fingers. They knew it was really she.

"Oh, golly! It's Caroline! It's Caroline!" Billy was so thrilled he could hardly speak. He didn't know what to say. He did a jig and looked at Susie in a way he had never looked at her before, and finally he gave her a quick hug.

"Susie found Caroline! Susie found Caroline!" he began to chant, and they started parading around the side of the house to tell Aunt Sally the good news. It reminded Susie of the parade in "Peter and the Wolf," the way they all marched along behind Billy in time with his chanting.

Uncle Gurney was away at work, but Aunt Sally came out and was delighted to see that Caroline had been found.

"Susie, that was wonderful, and I'm very proud of you. You weren't afraid to pick her up."

"Well, gee, Aunt Sally, there wasn't time to be afraid. In another second that old cat would have had her," said Susie, and was even surprised herself as she realized how true that was. There simply had not been time to be afraid.

Blake had been keeping in the background, but now Aunt Sally saw his mouth and his bruises.

"Blake Winthrop! Whatever happened to *you?*"

They told her about the fight. Aunt Sally cocked her head at Blake and pursed her lips.

"I suppose I can't scold you for fighting, if you were protecting your cousin."

"And Caroline," added Billy. "Don't forget about her. That big jerk wanted to put her in a jar of alcohol. I'd like to put *him* in one and see how he'd like it."

"Well, you come in here and wash that face before you go anywhere, young man," Aunt Sally told Blake. "You look disgraceful."

When Blake had washed his face, they started across the road with Caroline, to take her back to Billy's shed. But then they remembered.

"Hey! What are we going to put her in? The owl's still in her cage."

Billy looked at Caroline and Caroline looked at Billy. Neither one of them seemed to get an idea, but Blake did.

"Well, we ought to build Caroline a new cage anyway—but that will take time, so for now we ought to put her back in her old cage. Tell you what—the owl is well enough to be outside now, so why not put him in that old rabbit pen you've got out in back?"

"Good idea. Let's go."

As they started on, a car came down the road. It stopped beside them. Mr. Curtis looked out at them with a big grin. Mr. Curtis was the local druggist.

"Blake, I really enjoyed that fight."

"Gosh, Mr. Curtis, did you see it?"

"Sure. I was coming up the road and I stopped and watched. I guess you were too busy to notice me."

"I guess I was."

"That kid had it coming. He just got here today. He was in the drugstore this morning acting like a big shot all over the place. But do you know who he is?"

"No, Mr. Curtis, we never saw him before."

"Well, his name is Ray Schenley."

"Ray *Schenley*?"

"That's right, Blake. He's Beemis Schenley's nephew."

The Other Boy's Story

As Mr. Curtis drove away he was laughing loudly, but nobody else was. His words dropped like a bombshell among them and left them staring at each other dumbly. Of all people to have that boy turn out to be. Mr. Schenley's nephew!

"What will Mr. McGill say?" groaned Blake. "Well, I know one thing—I'm going straight back to the boat shop and tell him exactly what happened before anybody else tells him about it."

"Help me take care of Caroline and the owl and then we'll all go," said Billy. They hurried into the shed and Billy took the owl out of the cage. The bird turned its head almost all the way around to look at them, but it was quiet in Billy's hands.

"Put that bunch of branches in the pen so he'll have

something to sit on." Susie and Julia arranged several branches. The pen was covered with wire mesh on all sides and across the top. When Billy put the owl inside, it stretched its wings out once and then folded them. It walked up on a branch in the far corner and sat there staring at them.

"He'll be all right there," said Billy. Next they cleaned the cage and put Caroline inside. She seemed glad to be home again. Billy made sure the screen was securely in place. "Okay, everything's shipshape. Let's go."

When they walked into the shop, Mr. McGill was painting the bottom of a boat. He seemed surprised to see Blake again so soon. He eyed Blake's puffed lip curiously.

"What happened to your face, Blake?"

"That's what I came to tell you about, Mr. McGill. You see, Billy here lost a little snake and Susie found it and a boy tried to take it away from her and I stopped him and he hit me and—"

"Now, wait a minute." Mr. McGill held up his hands. "One thing at a time. What's all this about snakes?"

So Blake told him again, more slowly, and this time he understood.

"I didn't even know who the other boy was, because I'd never seen him before, but after the fight Mr. Curtis came along and he told us who it was."

"I see." Mr. McGill crouched down to paint alongside the keel of the boat. "And who was it?"

Blake cleared his throat nervously and braced himself against the workbench.

"It was a boy named Ray Schenley. I guess he's Mr. Schenley's nephew, or something."

Mr. McGill rolled back on his heels and sat down on the floor with a thump.

"What?" He rubbed a hand over his bald head and left a streak of copper paint on it. Then he rose to his feet, put down the paint brush, and walked to the door, staring out and muttering to himself. After a moment he pointed to an open convertible that was speeding toward them on the harbor road.

"Well, here comes Mr. Schenley, right on schedule. Blake, I guess it's just not meant for you to keep out of trouble with him."

"Gee, I sure don't want to have any more trouble with Mr. Schenley, but how was I to know that guy was his nephew? And what am I supposed to do, let him push my cousin around—a girl?"

Mr. McGill did not say anything. With his small figure framed by the big door, he watched silently as the car came closer. It swooped down beside the shop and skidded to a stop. Out climbed Mr. Schenley and his nephew Ray.

Mr. Schenley was wearing another yachting cap like the one he had lost in the water, and he had on his blue sea captain's jacket with the brass buttons.

Without saying anything, the children had moved back out of sight inside the shop. Blake looked as though for two cents he would have jumped out a window.

Mr. Schenley's voice was rasping with anger as he shook a warning finger at Mr. McGill.

"McGill, if you let that Winthrop kid set foot in this shop I'll never give you another penny's worth of business, even if I have to take my boats to Barnstable Harbor. Do you know what he's done now?"

"What's he done now?"

"He's grabbed my nephew off his bicycle and beat him up, that's what. Grabbed him from behind, never gave him a chance to fight back. Look at the boy's face! Look at that eye!"

Ray's face did look quite a bit worse than Blake's, it was true. He had a black eye.

"Not only that, he tore Ray's clothes!"

Mr. McGill stared at Ray, looking him up and down.

"Is that what happened, sonny? He grabbed you from behind, never gave you a chance?"

Ray scowled and looked away.

"Well, Ray?" said Mr. Schenley. "Isn't that what you told me?"

"That's right, Uncle Beemis."

Mr. McGill rubbed his hand hard over his bald head, smearing the paint on it, and began to grow grim around the mouth. Mr. McGill was slow to anger, but there were some things he could not tolerate.

"Grabbed you from behind, did he?" Mr. McGill turned and motioned to Blake. "Come here, Blake."

Blake looked frightened, but he walked out without hesitating and stood next to Mr. McGill.

Mr. McGill put his arm around Blake's shoulders and looked hard at Ray, who was staring popeyed at Blake.

"Do you want to repeat what you said, boy?" asked Mr. McGill.

Ray got over his first surprise enough to try to bluster his way out of the situation.

"I suppose you're going to believe anything he tells you," he sneered.

"I told the truth and I can prove it," said Blake, "because Mr. Curtis at the drugstore saw the whole fight. You were bullying my cousin Susie and that's why I fought you."

The other children edged into sight then, no longer frightened, and eager to back Blake's story if they had a chance.

Ray's mouth fell open and he could not seem to think of anything more to say. His uncle stared at him and

began to breathe heavily. Everyone was so quiet that Mr. Schenley's puffing sounded like a steam engine.

"Ray! Didn't you tell me the truth?" When Ray looked down at the ground and did not answer, Mr. Schenley pointed to the convertible. "Get in that car!"

Ray obeyed and slumped down in his seat, looking ashamed of himself. Mr. Schenley stamped around and slammed himself into the driver's seat. He started the motor with a great roar and drove away without another word. When the car had disappeared in a cloud of dust, Mr. McGill turned to Blake.

"Well, Blake, that settles that. You've got a job with me, no matter what Schenley does."

At suppertime they told Uncle Gurney all about everything that had happened that day. When they told him about the fight he took hold of Blake's chin between his thumb and forefinger and turned his face this way and that so he could get a good look at it.

"How did the other boy's face look?"

"He was a mess. He had a black eye."

"Attaboy," said Uncle Gurney.

"Gurney!" said Aunt Sally. "You shouldn't encourage the boy to fight."

"I certainly should. Any time anybody bothers his cousin, or his sister, I *expect* him to fight."

"Well, I suppose so," sighed Aunt Sally, because of course Uncle Gurney was right.

When supper was over, he sat back and said, "Well, now I want to go over and pay a call on Caroline. She might be hurt if I didn't welcome her back."

The children walked over with him. They found Billy sitting out by the rabbit pen looking at the owl.

"What's the matter, Billy?"

Billy shrugged his fat shoulders.

"Well, I was just wondering. I don't think he likes it very well in a cage, and I think his head is all right now. I was wondering if I ought to turn him loose."

They stood around the cage and peered in at the owl. He did look unhappy. Outside dusk would soon deepen into darkness. It was near the time when owls like to be flying around looking for a nice field mouse to have for dinner.

"Well, Billy," said Uncle Gurney, "I imagine if I were an owl I'd rather live in a hollow tree and be free than live in a cage and not be able to fly."

"It's different with Caroline," said Billy. "She doesn't want to fly."

"I doubt if she could, even if she wanted to," said Uncle Gurney. "I'll bet she's never even tried."

"Oh, Daddy!" said Julia, taking his hand. "You're so silly."

"Well," said Billy, "maybe I ought to let him loose."

He was sorry he could not keep the owl, but he had a respect for wild creatures and knew he would be wrong to make a captive of the bird. When he reached in the owl spread his wings and hissed at him, but he didn't bite. Billy waited, and then all at once he grasped the bird and brought him out of the cage. The owl blinked once and turned his head around.

Shadows lay long on the ground. There was a haze in

the air, and all the other birds had stopped singing and gone to sleep. Billy held the owl up in the air. It had curved its talons around his finger, and sat, balanced, staring at him with fierce round eyes.

"Well, old Mr. Owl, I guess you're all right now. So long," said Billy, and let go.

For a moment it sat like a carved statue, not a feather moving. Then it spread its wings and was gone. It didn't make the slightest sound. It simply vanished into the air.

"Good-by, old Mr. Owl," said Uncle Gurney. He turned toward the shed. "And now, lead me to my dear friend Caroline."

When she snuggled into bed that night, Susie thought about all the things that had happened. So much had gone on in such a few days. It seemed like a long, long time since she had first seen this room.

She thought about her mother and father and wished she could see them and tell them all about everything— but at the same time what she had told Aunt Sally earlier in the day was true: she had not had time to be homesick and unhappy. She had been too interested in what was going on. She had done things she had never expected to do, too. She had even picked up a snake. Of course, it was Caroline, and Caroline was really not so bad when you got used to her, but still she *was* a snake.

Not only that, but she had found a horseshoe crab in the sand out on the flats that afternoon, and she had picked it up by its spiky tail, after Blake had showed her that it couldn't hurt her. She was beginning to realize that a lot of things at the seashore were like that.

Moonlight was shining in the window, and by its pale light Susie could see the things Julia had collected in her room, all those things that spoke of the sea and had seemed so strange when she first arrived.

She could see the big conch shells on the dressing table, and the painted shell with the long spiky tail that was hanging on the wall, and the empty horseshoe crab.

The huge red lobster claw shone dully in the moonlight. Before she went home, Aunt Sally had promised to see that she had a big red lobster claw as a souvenir. She would hang it up in her room at home. Susie had never supposed she would want such a thing.

The fish-net curtains stirred in a gentle breeze, and as she lay very still she could hear the distant sound of the sea washing against the shore. It was a rhythmic, rolling sound, and it made her feel good without knowing why.

"Julia," she whispered, "can you hear the sea?"

Julia turned over.

"Yes," she whispered back. "I always listen when I get into bed."

They were silent then, listening together. After a

while from somewhere nearby they heard another sound.

"*Hoo-o-o-o-o!*"

Once upon a time a sound like that might have sent her head under the covers, but now Susie only chuckled.

"Do you think that's *our* owl, Julia?"

"I'll just bet it is. He's sitting out in a tree and telling us he's all right."

"And thanking us for helping him."

"*Hoo-oo-o-o-o!*" said the owl from some secret place in the shadows, away from the light of the moon. Julia giggled and made Susie laugh out loud.

"Julia, stop it. Aunt Sally will come up and get after us," she said, trying not to giggle herself. She thought about Julia and Blake and decided she liked them lots more than she had supposed she would. Even Billy Snow was all right after a while.

Her thoughts drifted sleepily to the *Argos*. She made a very earnest wish that Blake would be able to buy it by September. It would be terrible if Mr. Schenley bought it instead. She wished Blake had enough money right now, so he could be sure. Well, in the morning they were going to the wreck again to do some more digging. Maybe they would find something. Maybe they would find some real treasure. Maybe—

While she was still thinking about it, Susie fell fast asleep.

CHAPTER 15

Good News

WHEN THEY had finished breakfast, Uncle Gurney sat back from the table, looked fondly across at Blake, and said something tremendously exciting.

"Blake, your mother and I have been talking things over, and— Well, as you know, we had a lot of extra bills last winter and things were pretty tough for a while, but— Well, things are looking up some now, and by the end of the summer . . ."

Uncle Gurney stopped and grinned.

"What I'm trying to say is that if you stick to your jobs this summer and make as much money as you can, we'll put in the rest to buy the *Argos*."

Blake stared at his father as though he could not believe his ears. He jumped up and they all seemed to yell at once. Everybody hugged Uncle Gurney and each other while Tina ran around in circles barking joyfully as though she understood what everybody was so happy about.

"Golly, will I work now! Let me out of here—I've got a lawn to cut," cried Blake and rushed out of the house yelling for Billy so he could tell him the news before he went on over to mow the Underhills' lawn. Mr. Underhill was one of his regular customers.

The girls helped with the housework, but before long Aunt Sally caught Julia reading a book instead of dusting furniture. She swatted her once with a kitchen spatula and told them both to skat.

"Let's find out how near Blake is to being through," said Julia, as they rushed outside. "We'll walk and take the short cut."

"What short cut?"

"You'll see."

They went across the road and followed a narrow twisting path through the woods. The sun was blazing in a blue, blue sky, and every color that Susie saw seemed to have a special sheen. It was a perfect summer day. The girls were wearing shorts and polo shirts. Susie had on her blue sneakers. Julia was barefooted.

"How can you stand to go through the woods barefooted, Julia?"

"How can you stand to wear sneakers, Susie?"

Soon they came out on Spring Street, the center street

of the village, where the white church and the store were.
They went between two of the houses, which stood well
apart even in the center of the village, and took another
path through a thick stand of young elms. The path ram-
bled down a short slope and ran along the edge of a flat
carpet of thick green vines.

"Look at this, Susie. It's a cranberry bog."

"A cranberry bog? Right in the middle of the village?"

"Yes. It's a little one, but it's a real bog. They get fifty
boxes of cranberries from it sometimes, and three boxes
make a barrel. Those are the cranberry vines. You can
see the berries already beginning to grow. When it's fall
they'll turn red."

"I thought bogs were muddy places."

"Not cranberry bogs. They have sand all over them,
and most of the time they're nice and dry and sandy.
Look at this, Susie."

Julia had stooped down and was pointing to a flat round
plant the shape of a pincushion, its red blossoms so tiny
that it might have been a kind of moss. The blossoms
glistened as if they were wet.

"See how sticky it looks? Well it *is* sticky. That's so
it can catch flying insects. They light on it and stick to
it, and then it slowly eats them. It's a plant that eats
insects. And that's why it's good to have around cranberry
bogs."

Another patch of woods edged the other side of the bog. They passed through the woods and came out on Brook Street. Close by they heard a power lawnmower, and presently they saw Blake come around the corner of a house pushing the mower. He was whistling a merry tune and moving along as though it were no work at all.

When he had finished, he decided to walk down the hill to the harbor.

"Dad wants me to check his bait box for him," he said, but the girls knew he was thinking about the *Argos*, and they felt the same way. After he had put the lawnmower in a shed they started down the long hill.

"Look at her," said Blake, pointing to the sailboat as soon as she came in sight. Like a queen holding court, she sat at her mooring in the center of the harbor. The water was completely calm, and the boats were still in the water. Blake's eyes sparkled as he looked down at the *Argos*. "Just think, only twelve more weeks of mowing lawns and working at the boat shop and she'll be mine, and then we'll all go sailing every day."

"I won't. I won't be here," said Susie. She was not prepared for the rush of disappointment she felt as she remembered that by then she would be home again. In many ways it still seemed like a terribly long time before the summer's end, yet there was no question about one thing—she would like to go sailing every day in the *Argos*.

"Oh, gee, that's right. You'll have to leave before then. Well, we won't get to go sailing every day anyway, because there isn't enough breeze every single day," said Julia, trying to make her feel better.

"Well, maybe next year you can come back, Susie," said Blake.

It was nice of Blake to say that, of course, but Susie did not want anyone to think she would ever want to spend a summer away from home again.

"Oh, but I won't come back," she said quickly.

"Why not?"

"Well, my mother promised me I wouldn't have to come again if I didn't want to."

"But you want to, don't you? You like it here, don't you?" Julia sounded as if she could not imagine anyone not liking Cape Cod.

"Well, yes, I like it, in a way, but I hate being away from home for so long. You don't know what it's like to be away, Julia, you've never had to do it."

"Well, but after all, I don't have to go anywhere to spend the summer. I'm already here!"

Susie smiled.

"But Julia, there are other places where you could spend the summer. You make it sound as if this is the only place in the world."

"It's the only one for me."

"Me, too," said Blake. "Well, come on—as long as we're down here, let's row across and see what's going on at the boat shop."

"Gee, you can hardly wait to start there, can you?" asked Julia enviously.

As usual, Julia wanted to row, and she could not have chosen a better time to ask. Blake was in such a good mood he would have agreed to almost anything.

"Tell you what, you two sit side by side in the center and each work one oar. I'll sit in the stern and direct you. Now, if I want one of you to pull harder, I'll point to you. And Susie, be careful not to catch a crab."

"You mean you can catch crabs with your oars?" she asked nervously. Her cousins greeted this remark with scornful hoots.

"You sure can, but not the kind you think. Catching a crab is when you don't really get the blade of your oar into the water before you make your stroke."

"What happens then?"

"Well, when you do that you just hit the top of the water and splash it into the boat."

"Oh. Well, I'll be careful," said Susie. She and Julia started pulling on their oars.

"Together, now," said Blake. "Stroke . . . stroke . . . stroke . . ."

Susie carefully dipped her blade into the water, pulled

—and fell over backward in the boat as the oar slipped out of the oarlock.

"Hey, you've got to be careful not to pull up on it, Susie."

"I can see that now," she said, lifting herself back up onto the center seat, or thwart, as Blake called it.

"Try again."

"All right, now, Susie. Stroke . . . stroke . . ."

"We're going crooked," said Blake. "Pull harder on the starboard oar. That's you, Susie. Starboard is right, port is left. Pull harder!"

"All right, I . . . will!" said Susie, and pulled as hard as she could—only she was so busy thinking about pulling hard and not pulling up that she forgot about dipping the blade clear down into the water. With a smack she slapped a little wave right in the middle.

"Hey!" Blake tried to duck, but too late. If Susie had thrown a bucket of water she could not have done a better job of dousing him. He wiped his dripping face with his arm and shook a finger at Susie. "See? That's what I meant about catching a crab."

Both girls began to giggle because Blake looked so funny. Susie laughed so hard that she let go of her oar.

"Hey, watch it! Grab that oar!" yelled Blake, but it was too late. The oar had slid out of the oarlock and into the water and was floating away.

"I'll catch it, I'll catch it," cried Julia, and began to row as hard as she could.

"Julia, stop rowing! We're just going around in circles." Blake shouted angrily. "Here, give me that oar."

"Oh, all right, you always know so much—take it," Julia shouted back just as angrily. She lifted the oar out of the oarlock, but she was not watching what she was doing. The handle slipped out of her hand.

Now both oars were floating away.

"I think I can get it," cried Susie as Julia's oar floated past around the front of the boat. She leaned far over the side and made a desperate grab for it. Her fingers touched the oar—and then she felt herself slipping as the boat tilted under her.

"Blake!" she screamed, and then she had tumbled over the side into the water—water she knew was not only over her head, but very deep.

The water closed over her and she held her breath for dear life, beating her arms and legs around. It seemed as if she were going down and down; but instead she started to rise, and almost at once she popped to the surface.

As she did she heard a tremendous splash; Blake was in the water beside her.

"All right, Susie. Don't struggle, or I'll have to knock you out."

"I won't struggle," she managed to gasp. "Ow!" she cried, for Blake had grabbed her by the hair and was towing her back toward the boat.

"All right, now reach up and hold onto the gunwale, Susie, and stay here while I swim after the oars."

It felt very good to take hold of the edge of the boat—what Blake called the gunwale—and hang on. She had been terribly frightened. She looked up and saw Julia leaning over the side, grinning down at her.

"Gee, Susie, you looked funny. Your legs were straight up in the air. How's the water?"

Susie had been too busy to notice whether the water was warm or cold. Now she thought about it.

"Well, it's not bad," she had to admit. "It's not very cold at all."

A devilish gleam appeared in Julia's bright eyes. "I think I'm losing my balance, too. I think I'm falling in. Oh! Oh! I'm slipping!"

And before Susie could say anything, Julia had tumbled out of the boat and was in the water beside her.

"Julia!"

"Well, if you two are going to take a swim I'm certainly not going to sit in the boat."

"But you haven't got a bathing suit on; you've got shorts on."

"So have you."

"Yes, but I fell in!"

"So did I."

"But I didn't mean to."

"Well, I don't think Mommy will mind," said Julia, paddling around blissfully. "My, the water *is* nice, isn't it?"

"Julia, you really are crazy!"

"I am not. Look, Blake's got the oars."

Blake had caught up with the oars; and now he was swimming back against the current, towing them with one hand.

"I wish I could swim as well as Blake," Susie said as they watched him.

"Well, all you have to do is learn. Feel how easy it is to stay up in the water."

"How deep is it here?" Susie asked fearfully.

"Oh, I don't know. About a hundred feet."

"A hundred feet!"

Susie gasped and tried to climb into the boat, but her cousin broke into one of her silly giggles.

"I was only fooling. It's about twenty. But that doesn't matter. Daddy says it doesn't matter how much water is underneath you when you're only using the top part. See how easy it is to float? In fact, it's hard *not* to float. Wait till you try sometime to swim under water. Look at your legs right now. They're floating."

It was true, of course. Susie's legs were close to the surface of the water. She had a hard time keeping them down even when she tried, and the moment she relaxed they floated to the top again. She began to tread water, and she hardly had to hold on to the boat at all.

"Golly, when I get home and tell my mother and father I fell out of a boat!" she exclaimed, and all at once the water seemed more friendly than it ever had before.

"All right, now let's get in," said Blake. He put the oars in the boat and his head jerked around as he noticed his sister floating around on her back.

"Julia! What are you doing in the water?"

Julia blew water up in the air like a small whale.

"I fell in, too."

"You what?"

"The water looked so nice I fell in."

"On purpose, you mean."

"Well, yes."

"Mom ought to give you a whack," said Blake.

He pulled himself over the side of the boat and in. So did Julia. Then Susie tried it. She al-l-l-most made it, but each time her arms gave out and she slipped back down into the water.

"Gosh, what would I do if you weren't here to pull me in?" she asked.

"I don't know. Just hang there in the water until a shark came along and got you, I guess," said Blake with a nonchalant shrug.

"Hey! Help me out!"

"Don't worry," laughed Blake, "a shark would scrape his belly trying to come in here at low tide."

"But it's high tide now," Susie pointed out.

"Sharks wouldn't come in here any time. Here, give me your hand," said Blake, and with his help Susie was soon over the side and into the boat.

"Now we'll row on over to the boat shop," said Blake, "but this time *I'll* do the rowing."

CHAPTER **16**

Bad News

As BLAKE rowed back up the channel—for the current had carried them down it quite a way—they passed near the *Argos*. He edged toward her.

"Grab her rail—but hold us out so we won't rub against her," said Blake as he came carefully alongside. Already he was worrying about her paint as though he owned her. He looked up at the tall mast and then down at the cockpit.

"Captain Blake Winthrop of the *Argos*, that's what I'm going to be. Just ten more weeks, that's all."

"Gee, I wish . . ." Susie began, and then stopped as she realized what she was saying. Again she felt that stab of disappointment as she remembered that she would not be there to sail with them.

"Well, let's go on," said Blake finally. "Shove off."

When they reached the boat shop, they found Mr. Mc-

Gill at his workbench, surrounded by the parts of an outboard motor.

"Well, kids, no more bad news, I hope?"

"No, sir, I haven't even seen Mr. Schenley again," said Blake, and the man chuckled. "But I've got some wonderful news, Mr. McGill."

"That so?"

"Yes. If I make my hundred and ninety-two dollars working for you and mowing lawns all summer, Dad says he'll put in the difference so I can buy the *Argos*."

Mr. McGill stopped work to glance up at Blake, and his leathery face wrinkled up into a broad smile.

"Well, say. Well, what do you know. By George, I'm glad to hear it."

Blake's chest swelled with pride as Mr. McGill reached out and shook his hand.

"Congratulations, lad!"

"Thanks, Mr. McGill." Blake looked eagerly at the motor parts spread out on the workbench. "Can I help you with anything, sir?"

"Well, you can watch and learn, if you want to."

"Sure."

So Blake watched carefully while Mr. McGill worked on the motor and explained what he was doing. Motor parts strewn about on a workbench did not interest the girls very much, so they went outside and played in the sand. A car came down the road and turned in by the boat shop.

"That looks like Mr. Cartwright. You know—the man who owns the *Argos*," said Julia. "I wonder what he wants?"

"Let's go see."

Mr. Cartwright bounced out of his car and strode inside. He was chewing a big cigar more fiercely than ever, and he was scowling.

"Gee, I wonder what's eating Mr. Cartwright?" whispered Julia as they hurried along behind him.

"Let's hope he's mad at Mr. Schenley about something."

"Well, anyway, let's hope he's not mad at Blake."

The pair at the workbench glanced around as Mr. Cartwright came in. Both looked surprised at the expression on Mr. Cartwright's face.

"Hi, Mr. Cartwright," said Mr. McGill. "Something wrong?"

Mr. Cartwright let out an ill-humored groan.

"I'll say something is wrong. I'm so mad I could spit tacks."

"What's happened?"

"I thought I was all set for the summer, but no. Now suddenly they can't get along without me in Denver another week. They want me to come out right away."

Mr. McGill picked up a rag and wiped his hands on it, without paying much attention to what he was doing. He squinted sideways at Blake as though he were suddenly worried. Mr. Cartwright noticed Blake for the first time. An annoyed look crossed his face, as if he resented having to bother with Blake at that moment. But then he shrugged his shoulders heavily.

"Well, sonny, I'm just as glad you're here," he snapped. "Now, look here, this changes my plans. I can't fool around with that boat any more. I want to get clear of it and do it in a hurry. I don't want any loose ends when I leave here."

Under his tan, Blake's face had grown very white. He stood by the workbench, stiff and still.

Mr. Cartwright glanced around irritably, avoiding Blake's eyes.

"Now, Schenley's willing to pay me four hundred cash

for the *Argos*, and I'm going to have to take it. She's a
good boat, but she's old, and nobody else would pay a
price like that for her. Save your money and get a new
sailboat—"

"But a new one won't be as good, Mr. Cartwright!"
Blake burst out suddenly. "They don't make them as
good as that now."

"Yes, they do!" barked Mr. Cartwright, and then
looked away. Changing his tone, he continued, "Well,
I'll admit she's got something special, that boat, something it's hard to put your finger on, but just the same—
Well, that's how it is, sonny, and I haven't time to argue
or to fool around. I'm leaving here tomorrow, and I've
got a thousand things to do. I'm sorry, but that's life.
Believe me, I don't like the break I'm getting any better
than you like yours."

Mr. Cartwright turned around and strode angrily out
of the shop. As he reached the door he took the cigar
out of his mouth, scowled, and threw it away as though
it tasted bad. He turned and glowered at Blake.

"Tell you what I'll do. I'm leaving tomorrow morning. I won't sell the *Argos* until eight o'clock in the
morning, in case you manage to get together the money
somehow. But that's as long as I can wait."

With that, Mr. Cartwright turned on his heel, jumped
into his car, and drove away like a demon, with pebbles

rattling along the road as his wheels spun on the sand.

In the shop, nobody said anything. Blake walked to the door and stood with his back to them. His face twisted as he tried not to cry. Mr. McGill cleared his throat and looked as if he knew how Blake felt, because he understood what a boat could mean to a boy. Julia gulped and then let out a big sob, and Susie's lip quivered as two big tears rolled down her own cheeks.

Blake whirled around with his fists clenched, and his eyes were narrowed down to slits to hold back the tears.

"Just when everything was all set," he cried in a hoarse, quavering voice. "Oh, gosh. Gosh, Mr. McGill."

The man sat down on a box and shook his head in a sad way.

"Well, Blake, it's tough sometimes. Mr. Cartwright, now, he's upset because all of a sudden he has to leave and move to a new place. You'll find out, my boy—that's the way things work out sometimes in life. Lots of people are that way—when they're worrying about their own troubles, they don't care much about yours."

Blake walked up and down for a minute, moving as though everything about him hurt.

"Come on, let's go home," he said suddenly, and ran out of the shop. The girls looked at each other and followed him. He was already halfway to the beach. He turned to shout at them. "Let's go!"

They ran as fast as they could over the sand and through the occasional clumps of beach grass, and climbed into the dory without a word. Blake rowed across the harbor with hard, straining strokes. He never said a word, nor turned his head to left or right. Not once did he look in the direction of the *Argos* as they went by. Both the girls stole glances at it out of the corners of their eyes, and each time she did Susie felt worse.

Since they did not have their bicycles along they had to walk home.

"I'll go on ahead," said Blake gruffly, and hurried off. The girls did not try to keep up with him. They knew they could not.

"I guess he feels so bad he wants to get home in a hurry," Julia whispered.

It seemed like a long, long walk when they were so heavy-hearted. They watched Blake toil up the hill ahead of them. He looked small and lonely and dejected.

"Gee, Julia, what are we going to do?"

"I don't know, Susie. I can't think of anything. Can you?"

"No. But there must be *something*."

At home Aunt Sally was in the kitchen getting lunch ready. From the look on her usually cheerful face they knew Blake must have told her.

"You girls go up and get ready for lunch," she said quietly.

"All right. Oh, Mommy—"

"I know, Julia. It's too bad."

She put her arms around both of them and gave them a hug. "Be quiet when you go upstairs. Your father is having a talk with Blake."

"Oh." Julia beckoned to Susie and put her finger to her lips, and together they tiptoed up the stairs and into their

room. Julia went straight to the wall and put her ear
against it.

"Julia!" Susie was shocked, but Julia only touched her
finger to her lips again. Susie weakened. She put her ear
against the wall, too. They did so want to know what
Uncle Gurney and Blake were saying.

"But, Dad, Mr. Schenley's going to do awful things to
her. He's going to slap white paint all over her wood, and
he's going to spoil her rigging. He's going to ruin her."

"Son, if I could buy the *Argos* I would, but we can't
put that much money into a sailboat. Putting up part of
the money at the end of the summer season was one thing,
but putting up all of it right now is out of the question.
I'm sorry as I can be, but we simply can't afford it."

For a moment neither of them said anything more. The
girls listened breathlessly, and waited. They heard Blake
blow his nose loudly, and Julia whispered, "Gee, I'll bet
he's been crying."

"Well, I don't blame him," whispered Susie.

Blake was talking again.

"Yes, I know, Dad. But when I think about what Mr.
Schenley's going to do to her, I can hardly stand it."

Uncle Gurney sighed.

"People have to stand for a lot sometimes. All of us do.
I'm afraid you'll have to grit your teeth, son."

They talked some more, and presently Uncle Gurney

said, "Well, let's go down and have some lunch. Maybe that will make us feel better."

When they heard that, the girls rushed into the bathroom and began washing. Blake's door opened. He and Uncle Gurney came out looking very long-faced.

"Hello, girls."

Susie had never seen Uncle Gurney look so sad. He was usually chuckling and making jokes and having so much fun. Now he didn't look like himself at all.

Blake had his head down and didn't look at them. He and Uncle Gurney went on downstairs. As Susie dried her face on a towel she thought and thought.

"Julia," she said finally, "we're going to go and dig some more in the *Island Gull* this afternoon—anyway, that's what Blake said last night."

"Yes, but maybe he won't want to do it now. I don't guess he'll feel like doing much of anything."

"Sure he will. It's our only chance, Julia. We've *all* got to take shovels this time and we've all got to dig like we never dug before. Because we've *got* to find some treasure before tomorrow!"

CHAPTER 17

A Surprise at the Wreck

AT FIRST Blake felt too discouraged to want to dig at the shipwreck. Everybody had to urge him.

"The girls are right. You should go and dig some more. Even if you don't find anything, it'll be good for you. Better anyway than moping around the house," said Uncle Gurney. "Each of you get a shovel, and I'll give you a ride down to the burned cottage so you won't have to wrestle the shovels on your bikes. Is Billy going?"

"He said he would."

"Then go call him as soon as we finish lunch, and I'll take you down."

Before long the four children, each carrying a long-handled shovel, were walking across the sand dunes again toward the distant beach where the wreck was located.

Blake was far from hopeful.

"The trouble is, there's so much sand to shovel out of

the way before we can even see if there's anything left of the captain's cabin."

"Well, with all four of us digging at once, it'll make a difference," said Julia.

"Huh! Not much. It's still a lot of sand," Blake insisted gloomily. "I don't think we can shovel enough of it in one afternoon to really do any good."

They trudged up the last dune before the beach, and from the top of it they could look down at the wreck. Susie gained the top first, because she was the most eager and the most hopeful of them all. She felt sure they would find some kind of treasure.

Now she took one look at the wreck and was too surprised to move. She could hardly believe her eyes.

"Blake! Julia! Billy! Look!"

She pointed at the *Island Gull* as they raced up the dune. They were as astonished as she was.

"Criminee!" cried Billy. "What's going on there?"

"Who are all those people?" wondered Julia.

The *Island Gull* was crowded with people. They were climbing over her and walking around her and examining the timbers and the stern. They were all chattering at once. A whole row of shovels was stacked against the sandbank.

Rushing around the group like the most important ant in an anthill was a wisp of a man with a small gray mustache and gleaming spectacles perched on the end of his sharp nose. He was wearing a tweed jacket and what looked like old riding pants, leather puttees, and a wide-brimmed scoutmaster hat. He was acting like a scoutmaster, too. He seemed to be everywhere at once. He had a whistle hanging on a lanyard around his neck, and as they watched he blew a loud tweet on it. The people stopped and looked at him. Most of them were men, but there were several women in the group.

"Blake, what do you suppose they're doing there?" asked Susie.

"I don't know, but I'm sure going to find out. Let's go!"

They ran down the dune onto the beach, but began to feel shy as they drew nearer. There were so many people, all watching them approach. One man laughed and pointed at them.

"Well! Here come some recruits."

The little man with the riding pants and the puttees had his back to the children. He was about to speak to the group, but now he looked around and peered over the top of his spectacles at them.

"Well, well, well!" he said in a quick, chirping way. "Have you children come to help us dig?"

"Well, not exactly, sir," said Blake, scuffing at the sand with his sneaker. "We've been digging here before."

"Oh, so you're the ones."

"Yes, sir."

"We could see someone had been digging here. Well, good! Splendid! It makes me very happy to see young people interested in such things. Perhaps when you grow up you'll be members of our society."

"What society?" asked Blake, and the group laughed.

"Introduce us, Professor Kohler," one man suggested.

"Certainly. Children, we are members of the Southeastern Massachusetts Historical and Archeological Society," said the professor in a precise, fussy way, but with a twinkle in his eyes that made them smile. "Historical means we're interested in history. Archeological means we're interested in digging. When we heard about this old wreck being uncovered, we decided to have an outing on Cape Cod and take a look at it. We certainly hope you don't mind."

"Well, no," said Blake uncertainly. "It's just that—well, er—"

"Well?" Professor Kohler eyed him keenly. "What is the problem, lad?"

The professor reminded them of a small, busy bird, but there was something warm and kind about him in spite of his fidgety manner. You felt right away that you could trust him to be your friend. At least that was how he made Susie feel, so when Blake suddenly became shy and tongue-tied and could not seem to think of what to say, she blurted out an answer to the professor's question.

"We were digging for treasure!"

All the members of the Southeastern Massachusetts Historical and Archeological Society burst out laughing. All except the professor, that is. Blake glanced around darkly at Susie, as much as to say, "I told you so."

But Professor Kohler held up his hand to stop them.

"Now, now!" he said, wagging his head as though very sorry to hear what Susie had said. "Oh, dear! I had hoped you had your young minds on higher things, such as objects of historical interest. Instead you're grubbing for treasure."

"Well, we have a special reason," cried Julia.

"A special reason? What's that?"

Julia looked at Susie, and Susie looked at Billy, and they all looked at Blake. He was still embarrassed, but this time he managed to talk.

"Well, there's a sailboat we want to buy. We need four hundred dollars."

"So! So that's it."

"Well, come on," said one of the other men, grinning, "let's dig the wreck out and find some treasure for the kids. Let's form a company and split everything we find fifty-fifty—half for the kids and half for the Historical Society."

Blake's head came up at that, and his eyes grew wide. Susie knew he was thinking the same thing she was. He was looking at all those people and all those shovels.

"Golly, would you?" he asked, beginning to smile for the first time since they left the boat shop.

"Sure, why not? We came here to dig anyway, so let's dig. How about it, Professor Kohler?"

Professor Kohler looked at the beaming faces around him and lifted his whistle to his lips. He blew a shrill blast.

"Take shovels and prepare to board the wreck. We're about to start digging."

They all picked up their shovels and climbed into the sand-filled hulk. Professor Kohler darted around busily assigning people their "stations," as he called it, and directing operations with great enthusiasm.

"How about you children digging out around the stern some more? Will that be all right?" he asked.

"Anything you say, professor," Blake replied cheerfully. He was excited now. As for Susie, she was so thrilled she wanted to jump up and down and hug someone. With so many people digging, they would have all the sand out of the wreck in no time and then there was no telling what they might find.

Shovels flashed from all corners of the deck as sand poured over the sides, hitting the beach with a constant plop-plop-plop. The professor dug a little here, and a little there, and kept an eye on everything. After a while he stopped to gaze out at the sandbars that were beginning to show as the tide ran out.

"Going to be a good ebb today."

"That's right. You ought to come with us tomorrow morning, professor," said Blake. "Tonight's high tide is the highest of the year, so unless we have a bad wind we should have a very low tide tomorrow morning. We're going sea-clamming."

Susie stopped shoveling and stared at Blake in surprise.

"Gee, are we?"

"Yes. Dad said he'll take us all out."

"Oh, goody!" Julia clapped her hands and danced around her cousin. "Oh, Susie, will we have fun! I love to go sea-clamming better than almost anything."

"Well, I wish I could go with you myself," admitted the professor. "I haven't been sea-clamming for fifteen years."

One of the people on deck interrupted them.

"Professor Kohler, we've uncovered some deck planking."

The children dropped their shovels and followed the professor as he struggled up the sandbank to the deck.

Several wooden planks of the deck were showing near the back end. The professor dropped down on his hands and knees and examined everything carefully, nosing

around in a way that made Susie think of Tina sniffing a
scent.

"H'm! I do believe some of the cabin structure is left,
at that. Let's dig straight down here and see if we find any
vestiges of a vertical wall. Of course the whole space will
be filled with sand, but a few trinkets may be trapped. At
least it's worth an investigation, since we have so many
strong backs at our disposal."

Several of the men began digging where the professor had indicated. Before long the jagged edges of some upright boards were uncovered.

"Bring the screen," ordered the professor. Two men carried aboard a square wooden frame with a big piece of coarse screening nailed across it.

"We'll start sifting the sand now, in case anything turns up," said Professor Kohler. The diggers threw their sand onto the screen. A few pieces of wood appeared as the sand sifted through, but that was all. Then there was a metallic clinking sound, and a familiar object lay on the screen.

"Well. A spoon," said the professor, and examined it. He glanced at Blake and shook his head. "I'm afraid the captain's dinnerware was not very expensive. It's not silver."

Nothing else of interest turned up for a long time, but more men helped dig. Soon they had made such a deep hole that their heads were on a level with the deck. The space in the stern end of the ship, where the captain's cabin had probably been, began to take form.

Finally a piece of wood that had been turned and rounded appeared on the screen.

"This looks like part of a chair," declared the professor. Soon two more pieces of a chair came into sight as the sand sifted through the screen.

"Hey! Here's something," called one of the men who was shoveling down in the hole. "Here's a chest, and I think it's fastened to the floor and the wall. Anyway, it's right in a corner."

"Now, wait, wait!" cried the professor, as everybody started to crowd forward at once. "We can't all get down in there at the same time. Let me have a look at it. Perhaps we can pry it loose and bring it up."

Professor Kohler hopped into the hole with his coat tails flying.

"I hope this is your treasure, sonny," somebody said to Blake.

"Oh, I just know it is!" Susie told Julia. They squatted down to watch the professor examine the chest. Blake and Billy kneeled beside them. Blake was squeezing a handful of sand as hard as he could in each fist, trying his best to be patient.

"This is a transom," said the professor.

"A transom?" A lady in blue slacks raised her eyebrows. "I thought a transom was a window over a door."

"A transom can be several things. On a ship, it can be one of the timbers secured to the sternpost, such as these," he said, pointing to some wooden beams in the stern of the ship. "It can also be a seat built along the side of a ship's cabin. Such seats usually have drawers or a locker underneath."

"Does this one have any?"

"Well, let me see . . . Yes. The hasp that held it shut has corroded away, but obviously the top lifted up and the space under it was used for storage."

The professor straightened a bit creakily, brushed off his knees, and shot a glance up at Blake. "I don't want to disappoint you, but it's not likely we will find it full of gold doubloons, young man. It was more likely used for clothing or bedding, I'm afraid."

"Gee," muttered Blake, his face long again. Susie hoped fiercely that the professor would be wrong.

Professor Kohler turned back to the transom.

"I hardly think it's worth preserving, so we may as well break it open where it stands. It will be full of sand, of course. Sand will fill up anything as long as there's the slightest chink. Throw a sock into the sea, and when it washes up on the beach it will be full of sand. If an old pair of pants comes ashore, its pockets will invariably have sand in them. Well, now, let's have a look."

The hinges on the transom had corroded away like the hasp, so that the top came off easily as the men pried it up with their shovels. Inside, just as Professor Kohler had said, was sand.

"Now then, let's scoop this out with our hands. Give us the screen down here."

The professor and another man began scooping out the

sand and dropping it on the screen while two other men held the frame level. At first nothing appeared. Professor Kohler ran his fingers carefully through a handful of sand and separated a few shreds of cloth from it.

"H'm. Barely recognizable, but I think this was once linen. I wonder if the captain slept between linen sheets?"

They continued to work and found more shreds of brown cloth. Susie's spirits sank lower. Still, maybe at the very bottom there would be something.

Even as she was thinking how much she wished the professor would be wrong, and the bottom of the chest would be full of gold doubloons, the professor spoke again.

"Here. Here's something."

"I feel something, too," said the other man.

When the sand had fallen through the wire mesh, they saw that four large round objects lay on the screen.

Professor Kohler picked one up and studied it carefully, tilting his head back to look through his spectacles. Then he glanced up at Blake with a disappointed expression on his thin, leathery face.

"Buttons," he said.

They all examined the buttons, passing them from hand to hand. Professor Kohler said they were probably from a jacket.

That was as close as they came to finding anything in the transom.

The professor took out a tape measure, checked the dimensions of the cabin, and made notes. Two of the ladies and one man made sketches of the way the stern was constructed and of the wreck as a whole. Others took photographs. A few dug some more, but they found nothing of interest.

"Well, it's getting late. We should think about starting back," the professor said when he had completed his measurements. "Some of us have quite a way to go."

He turned to the children and cocked an eye at each of them in turn.

"Well, I'm sorry we didn't find any treasure for you, but I'm afraid the old *Island Gull* simply wasn't that kind of ship. I hope you work it out some other way to buy your sailboat."

The professor waved his arms busily and blew his whistle.

"Gather up all shovels and count them—and be sure to get everything else."

The members of the Society collected the shovels and the screen, the thermos bottles and sketching pads and hats and sunglasses they had brought along. A moment later they were crossing the dunes in a long, straggling column, heading for the place where their cars were parked. The professor was the last to leave. He hopped about making sure that nobody had left anything behind.

He reminded Susie of a turnstone, one of those little birds that bustles around on the beach turning over shells and stones with its bill.

When everything had been done to his satisfaction and he had one last look around, the professor pattered away briskly over the dunes to catch up with the others. Just before he crossed the top of the last dune he suddenly pivoted, craned his neck back at them, and waved good-by.

"Good-by!" The children waved until his head bobbed out of sight. With heavy hearts they turned and started back across the dunes in the direction of the village.

"He was nice," sighed Susie.

"Who?"

"The professor."

"Oh. Yes, he was okay. He tried to help us, anyway."

At the top of the dune they stopped to look back at the wreck. It was alone on the beach now, and it seemed forlorn and deserted. All around it were footprints and piles of sand.

Blake sat down as though he were dead tired. His face was filled with complete despair as he gazed at the wreck.

"Our poor old treasure ship," he said in a low voice. "It was our last chance, and now even that chance is gone. Now we'll never sail in the *Argos* again."

CHAPTER **18**

Danger on the Flats

Susie found it difficult to go to sleep that night. For one thing, they went to bed early because they were getting up at dawn to go sea-clamming with Uncle Gurney. And the other thing was that Susie dreaded going to sleep, because when she woke up it would be morning—the morning when Mr. Cartwright was going to sell the *Argos* to Mr. Schenley. She did not want that morning to come.

The last time she felt that way had been the night before she left home to come to Cape Cod for the summer. She had thought that was the worst feeling she could have, but this one was just as bad.

She tried her best to stay awake so that the time would not pass so fast, but finally she began to be sleepy. The next thing she knew someone was shaking her and whispering, "Susie. Susie. It's time to get up."

Susie's eyes flew open and she saw Julia standing by her bed.

"What time is it, Julia?"

"It's a little past four o'clock."

"Oh! Well, at least it isn't eight o'clock yet."

"No. Not yet. It's still dark outside. Be very quiet, because Mommy isn't going, and she's still asleep."

"What shall I wear?"

"Wear your swim suit, so you won't have to worry if you get wet."

Susie followed this suggestion, and Julia waited while she put on her blue sneakers. Julia was going barefoot, of course. But Susie couldn't help it; she could not bear the thought of walking across the wet sand flats in bare feet.

When Susie was ready they tiptoed downstairs. Uncle Gurney had prepared breakfast. Blake was sitting silently at the table.

They ate quickly and went outside, eager to start. Blake put some buckets in the back of the station wagon, and also some rakes with long curved teeth. They would use these for digging up the sea clams, Julia explained.

They drove down a sandy road that went past the village cemetery and on through scrubby woods and brambly fields until it reached a high point above the beach. It was still dark and there was not a sound to be heard except the swish of the tires on the sand road.

The car headlights lit up the road, but otherwise it was so dark that Susie could only see the black, shadowy outlines of the trees that crowded down to the edge of the road.

"Susie, I want to explain to you about sea-clamming," said Uncle Gurney. "First of all, the sea clam is as big as my two hands. Well, you've seen the shells, so you know how big they are."

"Yes, Julia has shown me the shells, Uncle Gurney."

"Good. Now, when you grind up the meat of the sea clam, it's very good to eat, either in a chowder, which is a kind of soup, or in a sea clam pie. If we get a lot of sea clams, your Aunt Sally will make us a sea clam pie."

"And sea clam pies are yummy," said Julia.

"They certainly are. Well, so that's what a sea clam is. The next thing is, how do we get them?"

"Julia says you can only get them once a month, at the time when the tides are the very lowest."

"That's right. The higher the tide is when it comes in, the lower it is when it goes out. Six hours after a very high tide, we have a very low tide. The farther out the tide goes, the more the sand flats near the shore are exposed. And away out on the edge of the sand flats live the sea clams, down in the sand."

"But how do you know where to dig? There's an awful lot of sand."

"On a good tide the sea clams 'show.' That's what we call it. They show where they are by leaving little marks in the sand above their hiding places. You have to look for those little marks and dig where you see them. They look something like thumbprints. If you disturb a sea clam he will squirt water up through the sand. So one thing we will do is to stamp our feet as we walk along."

"Stamp our feet?"

"Yes. That way we'll hope to disturb the clams, so that they will squirt and show us where they are. You know how it disturbs me to have you girls stamp around in your room when I'm downstairs trying to read the paper?"

"Yes."

"Well, sea clams are like me. It disturbs them to have anybody stamping around upstairs. The only difference is, I don't squirt water at you. I yell at you instead."

"That's right, Daddy," said Julia.

"Well, I hope we find some sea clams," said Susie.

"I hope so, too, but I don't like the way this breeze is coming up from the northeast." Uncle Gurney glanced out at the trees and bushes that were moving slightly in a fitful breeze. "I'm afraid we may get some rain. My, but it's dark. Usually sea-clamming tides come at the time of the full moon and we have a bright moon to light our way until dawn, but this tide came at the time of the new moon, and that's why it's dark. Of course, with this kind of weather it would be so cloudy that we couldn't see the moon anyway."

During all the ride, Blake had not said a word. They all knew what he was thinking about. In only three hours, the *Argos* would belong to Mr. Schenley.

When they reached the point of land above the beach where they were to leave the car, it was no longer pitch dark, but neither was the sky growing much lighter. It was cloudy and sullen.

"Oh, say can you see, by the dawn's early light?" Uncle Gurney sang the first line of "The Star Spangled Banner" and shook his head. "I'm afraid we're not going to get much dawn's early light this morning, with all these clouds."

It looked cold and cheerless in the open on such a dismal morning. The sand flats melted away into the darkness, vast and forbidding.

Everybody took a bucket and a rake and started down the hill to the beach. The dew on the beach grass was cold against her legs, but otherwise Susie was surprised to find that it was not actually so chilly after all.

In the gloomy light the sand was wet and dark. There were pools of water here and there which felt warm when they waded through them. Susie started as she felt a squirt of cold water hit her legs, but Uncle Gurney reassured her.

"Razor clams. They squirt straight up in the air, like

sea clams. If you feel any cold water squirted on you when we get to the sandbars, stop and dig, because out there it will be a sea clam."

They passed a line of wooden poles used by the fishermen to mark a weir. They walked and walked and walked, and still the flats spread out before them, silent and empty. A breeze stirred now and then, and the air was full of moisture. They came to channels in the sand through which water was running with a strong current. In one the water nearly reached Susie's waist as she waded across.

"How far is it to the outer bars, Uncle Gurney?"

"Over a mile, Susie. It's quite a walk, but it's wonderful out here. The whole world seems to stretch away from you in every direction. It's like no place else I know of."

"It makes you feel so *little*," said Susie, and her uncle nodded.

"That's right. But that can be a good feeling sometimes."

They could hear the lap-lap-lap of rippling waves rolling onto the outer bars now. The sound came closer and closer. Susie could see the white line, away in the distance, where the water foamed onto the sand. Still they walked and it didn't seem to get any closer. A couple of seagulls wheeled past overhead, looking for their breakfast, and a flock of small birds came flying along swiftly just a few feet above the sand, swinging toward the water.

"The seashore is beginning to wake up," said Uncle Gurney.

Again a stream of cold water splashed Susie's leg and made her jump.

"Uncle Gurney! I got squirted again."

"Let's have a look. Ah. See here." He pointed at the sand, alongside one of Susie's footprints. "See that mark, sort of like a thumbprint, with a little hole at the edge of it? That's where our friend is. Now, take your clam rake and dig down there about six inches and see if you hit anything."

Susie thrust her rake into the sand, and felt it touch something solid. At the same moment another fountain of water squirted out of the hole in the sand.

"That's him. Dig him up."

Susie dug and finally worked the prongs of her rake under what felt like a large stone. She pulled it up, and there on the sand lay an enormous clam with a dark blue shell.

"He's a dandy. We're off to a good start," said Uncle Gurney. "From now on let's all keep our eyes open."

"Can I put him in my bucket, Uncle Gurney?"

"Certainly. He's your clam."

"Can I pick him up?"

"He won't bite you, if that's what you mean. But at the same time, if he opens his shell don't stick your finger in, because he can clamp down tightly."

Susie lifted the clam gingerly and put him in her bucket. He made a loud thump. He was heavy. Susie grinned proudly.

"That was fun. My first clam. Let's find some more."

From then on they watched carefully and stopped to dig every few feet, but no more clams were discovered until they reached the outer bar. There they began to find more. Susie located three, although many times when she dug she found nothing. It took a sharp eye to see the true marks. Uncle Gurney said she was his star pupil.

Julia had a good time but she did not find as many clams as Susie because she ran around chasing birds and looking for crabs in the surf and making patterns in the sand with her rake. Blake poked off by himself, but at least he did search for clams, and soon he had several in his bucket.

Susie was enjoying herself and hoped they could stay for a long time. The only trouble was that Uncle Gurney was worrying more and more about the weather.

"I'm afraid we'll have to go in pretty quickly now. I hate to do it, but I'm sure it's going to storm. We ought to get started back to shore before the tide turns, too, because when it turns today it will probably come in pretty fast."

He called them together and they found that between them they had over two buckets of clams.

"We have all we need, so let's start in."

"Let's divide them up in the four buckets, Dad, and I'll take two and you can take two. That way it won't be so hard to carry them." Blake explained this to Susie. "When we do that we're balanced, with something in each hand."

"Oh, I see." They were all glad to hear Blake say something. He had been so downcast all morning.

Uncle Gurney took two buckets, and Julia carried his rake and hers. Susie took Blake's rake, and he picked up the other two buckets. They followed Uncle Gurney and Julia.

As she thought of how far it was back to shore, Susie

realized that her feet hurt. Her sneakers had a lot of sand in them, and they were very uncomfortable.

"Wait, I've got to empty my shoes before I walk any more."

Blake set the buckets down and looked at her impatiently.

"Aw, Susie, if you'd just take 'em off and walk barefoot instead of being such a sissy you wouldn't have any trouble and that's a fact."

"Well, I don't want to take them off and I'm not going to and *that's* a fact," Susie retorted tartly. She hated to have Blake call her a sissy. She threw the rakes aside angrily and sat down in the sand.

Clank!

The prongs of one of the rakes stuck something.

"Hey, take it easy with those rakes."

"I'm sorry," mumbled Susie. Blake looked to see what they had hit.

"Say, what's this?" He commenced to dig in the sand. A black piece of metal was sticking up and as he dug they saw that it was the corner of a small flat case or box. Susie jumped to her feet and came over for a closer look as Blake dug it up.

It was a metal box about a foot long and six inches wide and three inches deep.

They stared at each other with round eyes.

"Blake! Maybe *this* is a treasure box!" cried Susie. "It's so heavy!"

Blake wanted to believe it, but he had been disappointed too often.

"Huh! It's heavy because it's full of sand, that's all. See that little hole? That was probably a keyhole, and that's where the sand got in. Let's see if I can get it open."

He could not budge it, however.

"Well, let's at least take it in with us," said Susie. "You know what Professor Kohler said. He said there might be parts of the *Island Gull* buried all over the flats. Maybe this is from the *Island Gull*. I can carry it."

"It's pretty heavy."

"That's all right. Why, it's not bad at all," said Susie, lifting it to see. She put the box down and sat on the sand again.

"First, though, I've got to empty my shoes."

"Okay, but hurry. If we don't get going, Dad will be worried about us."

"Then you start on ahead."

"Well, maybe I'd better. You just follow my tracks right in. And don't be long."

"I won't."

Blake looked down at the box and his eyes lighted up for the first time.

"Golly, Susie, wouldn't it be wonderful if . . ."

"Oh, Blake, I hope so! What time is it now, do you think?"

"About six o'clock."

"Then there would still be time."

"Yes." Blake looked yearningly at the box, and then shrugged. "Oh, it's crazy. I'll bet you there's nothing in that box but sand."

He picked up the two buckets. "Can you carry the rakes, too, all right, Susie?"

"Sure."

"Then I'll get started. You come on just as soon as you've emptied your shoes."

"All right, Blake."

Susie watched him walk away, and then she took off one sneaker. The sand was so wet that it stuck. It clung to the inside of the shoe. She had to pick the last of it out one grain at a time.

She felt comfortable sitting there on the sand, and she worked slowly. When she finally finished the job to her satisfaction and had her sneakers on again, Blake was a tiny figure in the distance. She picked up the box and then remembered the rakes.

"Oh, heck." Having the rakes, too, made it very awkward. She had to carry the box in one arm and hold the two rakes in the other hand.

She had not gone very far before she realized the box was heavier than she had thought. The farther she walked the heavier it grew, until she decided she would have to stop and rest for a minute.

Susie set the box and the rakes on the sand and stretched her back. It was wonderful to stop and rest. She could still see Blake in the distance, but just barely. He looked miles and miles away.

She noticed what looked like a sea clam's mark and remembered how she had found one on the way out. She dug and sure enough there it was.

"Well, I can't carry you, but it was fun to dig you up anyway. Now you can dig yourself right back in."

She looked around to see if there were any more marks, wandering around in circles with her head down.

Suddenly it began to rain, and not a light rain, either. It was a violent cloudburst. Susie looked up, and all she could see was a gray curtain of rain. There was no sign of

Blake. In fact, she had been walking in circles so much that now she did not even know where the shore was. It looked the same in every direction.

She found the box and the rakes and peered around for Blake's tracks, wiping her eyes as rain splashed into them. But she had not been following too carefully, because she had been able to see Blake himself. And now the tracks had disappeared.

"Blake! Blake!" Susie wanted to run, but she knew she must not until she was sure she was running in the right direction. For all she knew, she might be running straight toward the sea instead of the shore. What was more, the tide was coming in now, and the water was rising. If she did not get to shore soon, it would rise and rise until finally it would be over her head.

Susie saw how the sea was beginning to seep into the low places. It filled the furrows in the sand with long fingers of water. All around her the fingers began reaching toward her, as though they were trying to catch her. Susie sobbed with terror, and almost dropped the box and rakes. She wanted to run—but she stopped. She hugged the heavy box to her. *Nothing* was going to make her let go of it! All at once, because she had the box to worry about, she was over being so terrified. She began to think hard.

"I've got to find Blake's tracks somehow," she said aloud. "I've got to."

CHAPTER 19

The Shore--or the Sea?

SUSIE QUICKENED her step, walking as fast as she could, watching for any sign of tracks. She walked in the direction that felt the most like the right one, but she was not at all sure of it.

As she walked the box became heavier and heavier and the rakes more and more unwieldy. Twice they nearly tripped her. The rain drummed on the flats, blotting out all signs. The furrows filled in completely, and in some places she was ankle deep in water. She began to cry as she saw how, all around her, the flats were disappearing and becoming a solid sheet of water, with only the ridges of a few sandbars showing.

She wiped her eyes and tried to forget how frightened she was. It didn't help to have her eyes blurred with tears. She kept hoping for footprints, but now that most of the flats were under water any such hope became increasingly forlorn. She stumbled on, searching wildly for something that would tell her whether she was headed for shore.

Once she stepped into a deep place and fell forward, dropping the box and the rakes and skinning her knees. For a moment, as she stood sobbing in the rain, with the water swirling about her feet, she felt she could not carry the box another step. But then she gathered up the rakes, picked up the box, and started on again.

The rain let up slightly and she could see a little farther around her, but even that did not help much. Her arms ached and the backs of her sneakers ground sand into her heels so that every step she took made her limp.

She was plodding along, ready to cry again, when, a few yards ahead of her, sticking up out of the sand, she saw the broken-off end of a wooden pole. She ran toward it.

There were more poles in each direction, gleaming darkly in the rain.

Now she knew she must be going the right way, because they had passed the line of poles coming out.

She hurried from pole to pole, forgetting her aches and her sore feet in the joy of being safe—until suddenly she heard running water.

Was it the sea? Had she come in the wrong direction after all? Had she gone toward the sea instead of toward the shore?

On trembling legs Susie walked a few steps more onto

the top of a sandbar—and saw a rush of water going past.

It was a channel, and she was sure it was one of those they had crossed on the way out. But because of the way the water had risen, it was hard to tell how wide it actually was, or how deep in the middle. She knew she could not wade across it, and certainly she could never get across it at all if she tried to carry the box and the rakes.

Had she carried the box this endless distance only to have to abandon it? She looked around despairingly, trying to find a solution.

The wooden poles gave her an idea. She would leave the box by one of them, and Blake would be able to find it again.

That took care of the box, but what about the rakes? If only she could tie the rakes to the pole, she could save them, too—except that she had no rope or string.

Susie stared down at her blue sneakers. Her shoe-laces! But if she took them out of her shoes she would not be able to keep her sneakers on.

Just as when she had rescued Caroline, there was no time for being scared. Susie struggled with the wet laces and finally pulled them out. Then came the worst part of all—taking off her sneakers. Her toes curled as she stepped into the water with her bare feet. She kept telling herself that nothing was going to bite her, nothing was going to hurt her. Quickly she tied the rakes to the pole, shivering as the rain beat down on her with renewed violence.

Now she had her sneakers to carry. Well, at least there was one easy way to get *them* across the channel. She could throw them.

Her heart sank as she gazed across the stretch of rushing water. It was impossible to tell exactly how wide it was. The sandbar on the other side was completely out of sight.

Susie threw one sneaker as hard as she could. It plopped into the water on the far side and disappeared, beyond the range of the current in the channel. She threw the other, and it plunged out of sight, too. Then she approached the channel and took a deep breath, screwing up her courage. Just a few kicks and she should be across the deep part in the middle. She had to take a chance.

Susie waded in, held her breath, and pushed out into the stream. She began kicking as vigorously as she could and dog paddling. The strong current swept her along until she was flung against the opposite bank of the sandbar, scratching her chin on the sand. She was across.

She scrambled out and recovered her sneakers, which were in shallow water close by. Running beside the line of poles, she felt as light as air, and she laughed with relief. The weather seemed to surrender and admit she had won. The rain lessened. The sky grew lighter. And from nearby she heard Blake's voice.

"Susie! Su-u-u-sie!"

"Blake!"

She stopped and shouted as loud as she could. Blake appeared out of the rain a short distance away.

"Susie! Gee, I thought you'd got lost."

"I did. Oh, Blake, I was scared."

"So was I!"

"Listen, I left the box back there by one of the poles. And I tied the rakes to the pole, too."

"How far back?"

"Not very far."

"I'll go get them. Wait right here. We're not far from shore, so you're safe." Blake dashed away through the slackening downpour, following the line of the poles.

It seemed to Susie he would never get back. But he did, and when he appeared he was carrying the box and the rakes.

"I got 'em. Let's go."

"Where are your buckets?"

"They're close to the beach. I know just where I left them, don't worry. But when I got near the beach I wondered if you were all right, so I came back to make sure."

By the time they reached the shore the rain had become a mere spatter of drops. They could see Uncle Gurney and Julia watching for them. Uncle Gurney rushed out with a wild-eyed expression, and it was difficult to tell whether he intended to hug them or knock their heads together.

"Where have you two been?" he cried, speaking in the loud, angry way fathers do at such times. He put an arm around each of them as though to make sure they were really there. "I thought—I was afraid that— What took you so long?"

They told him as they walked back to the car. Before they were through he was chuckling and shaking his head and saying he had heard of some crazy doings, but this beat them all.

"That's quite a box," he said, when they showed it to him. "H'm. We'll have to take it to my workbench to open it, I imagine."

When they came up the walk at home looking like four drowned rats, Aunt Sally gave them all a scolding for staying out in such bad weather and making her uneasy. While they watched Uncle Gurney and Blake try to open the box they told her what had happened.

After two or three tries, Uncle Gurney managed to pry the top off the box. They crowded around to look into it.

As Blake had predicted, it was brimful of sand.

They carefully scooped this out and shook it through a piece of screen into a pan, but nothing interesting turned up. Nothing at all.

Blake's shoulders sagged, but he pretended not to be disappointed. "Shucks, I knew there wouldn't be anything in it anyway."

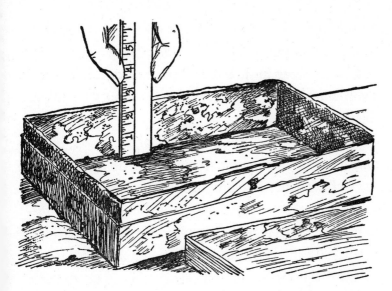

Susie stared at the box, and tears blurred her eyes. After all the struggle they had gone through, after the way she had carried it until her arms ached and her back ached, it was terrible to have it be empty.

Uncle Gurney was studying the box closely. His face had become thoughtful.

"You know, this might have been a money box of some kind," he murmured, "and boxes like this some-times had a trick to them. Hand me that ruler, Blake."

Carefully he measured the inside depth of the box. Next he measured the outside.

"Yes, sir. Look at this. This box is three inches deep on the outside—and only two and a half inches deep on the inside. It's got a false bottom."

"Oh, golly, Dad. Do you mean it?"

"Now, don't get excited, son. That doesn't mean there will be anything in it. But at least it does have a secret compartment and— Hand me that chisel and let's get this thing open."

Uncle Gurney banged away with mighty blows, beginning to look eager himself. The box gave up its secret. He was right. There was more space under the false bottom.

In that space there was more sand, but there was something else, too. There were small round discs.

Uncle Gurney took one and cleaned it off with a rag.

"Hey!" He cleaned it some more, rubbing rapidly, and then examined the disc again.

It was a coin.

He put it aside and dug out the others, one by one.

"What is it, Dad?"

"Just a minute."

Before long there were fourteen coins piled on the workbench, all rubbed clean enough to be identified.

"What are they, Gurney?" asked Aunt Sally, unable to stand the suspense any longer.

"I just wanted to make sure before I said anything," he told her. He held up one of the coins and it gleamed dully in the light. "It needs more polishing—but it's a perfectly good U.S. twenty-dollar gold piece."

Susie felt as if the basement walls would be blown out

by the explosion of joy that shook them. Five voices whooped in unison, followed by the kind of happy confusion that always occurs when five persons of different heights and sizes all try to throw their arms around each other at once. Susie and Julia screamed into each other's white faces and came together as roughly as two bear cubs. They were dancing around all over one another's feet when Blake thought of something that sobered them.

"Wait a minute! How many are there, Dad? Fourteen?" The joy faded from his face. "But that's only two hundred and eighty dollars. That's not enough."

Uncle Gurney put a hand on his son's shoulder. He turned to Aunt Sally.

"Sally, we can't let him lose out now. We shouldn't do it—our bank account doesn't justify it—but just the same, I'm going to put in the rest."

Blake looked at Uncle Gurney as if he were the greatest man on earth.

"Dad! Will you?"

"Yes."

Blake's arms went around his father and he hid his face for a moment. But then Uncle Gurney thought of something that caused a new explosion.

"Say! What time is it, anyway?"

Aunt Sally stared at her watch.

"Good heavens! It's five minutes of eight!"

CHAPTER 20

Hold Everything!

I⊤ was surprising that none of them was trampled underfoot on the basement steps, because they all tried to reach them at once.

"The telephone! Call Cartwright!" shouted Uncle Gurney. "No, I'll do it myself. Let me at that phone."

He rushed to the telephone and shouted at the operator.

"Give me Mr. Cartwright! I don't know his number, but— What? The line's busy?"

Uncle Gurney slammed the phone down with a groan.

"He's on a party line, and the line's busy. Somebody else is on the line. Well, we can't wait. If we jump in the car we may be able to make it in five minutes. Let's go."

They rushed out to the car. Billy Snow was just coming out of his house.

"Come on, Billy."

"What's up, Blake?"

"Never mind—jump in!"

"My checkbook! My checkbook!" Uncle Gurney suddenly remembered that he was only wearing swimming trunks and an old shirt. Aunt Sally raced back to get it.

They went out of the driveway on two wheels.

"For heaven's sake, don't kill us all before we get there, Gurney!"

"I just hope Cartwright's clock agrees with ours, Sally. Blake, have you got those coins?"

"Sure, Dad." Blake held up a jar. It had been sitting on the workbench with some screws in it. Now it contained the gold coins.

"Well, hang onto it." Uncle Gurney swung onto the highway. Mr. Cartwright lived on the other side of the harbor. In order to get to his house they had to drive up the highway about a mile and then turn into another road. Uncle Gurney drove as fast as he could without going over the speed limit.

"What time is it now, Mom?" asked Blake, as they turned off the highway.

"One minute to eight."

"Oh, I hope Mr. Cartwright waited!"

"We'll soon know. Here's his house," said Uncle Gurney. A big convertible was parked ahead of them in the circular drive.

"That's Mr. Schenley's car," cried Blake.

"So he's here, all right," said Uncle Gurney, as he swerved in and screeched to a halt behind the convertible.

"Hurry!"

They piled out as fast as they could, and Blake ran to the door of the house with Uncle Gurney close behind him. The windows were open, and they could hear Mr. Schenley talking in his loud voice.

"Listen, Cartwright, this is silly. You know as well as I do that boy isn't going to turn up here with any four hundred dollars. Take my check, and let's call it a deal."

"Look, Schenley, I told him I'd wait until eight and I'm going to wait, even though—"

"Mr. Cartwright!" Uncle Gurney called out firmly and knocked on the door.

Mr. Cartwright came to the door and stared out at them. He was so surprised his cigar almost fell out of his mouth.

"Why—why, hello, Winthrop. Come in."

They walked in. When Mr. Schenley saw who it was his eyes nearly popped out of their pouches.

"Mr. Cartwright, will you accept United States gold coins in part payment for the *Argos*? I'll give you my check for the balance."

Uncle Gurney motioned to Blake.

"Pour them out on the table, son."

Blake poured them out of the jar onto a table. With an

astonished look on his face, Mr. Cartwright picked one up and examined it.

"By George! A twenty-dollar gold piece. Where did you get them?"

Blake told him exactly what had happened. Even Mr. Schenley listened without interrupting. He seemed too surprised even to protest.

"Will you accept them, plus my check for the difference, Mr. Cartwright?"

Mr. Cartwright chewed his cigar back and forth, and clinked the coins together.

"I don't see why not. They're legal tender. Sure I will."

At that point Mr. Schenley found his tongue again.

"Oh, now, wait a minute, Cartwright! You can't back out on our deal now."

"I'm not backing out on any deal, Schenley. I told you

this boy had first chance. I gave him until eight o'clock this morning to buy the *Argos*. It's eight o'clock, and he's here with the money. If you ask me, I think the good Lord intended him to have the boat, and personally I'm glad he's getting her, because he's the best young sailor I've seen around here."

Mr. Schenley's face was red, but he saw that he could not bully Mr. Cartwright into changing his mind. He picked up his yachting cap and jammed it on his bald head.

"All right! All right, if that's the way you want it. Why should I bother with that old tub, anyway? I'll buy a *new* sailboat, the finest one this place has ever seen, and I'll back the *Argos* right off the map!" Giving them a haughty look, Mr. Schenley turned and strutted out the door.

Mr. Cartwright snorted. "The day you outsail this boy in *any* boat, Schenley, I want to be here to see it."

Mr. Schenley spun around as though stung. Then without a word he jumped into his car and went roaring away up the road.

"It's good for him not to get his way for once," growled Mr. Cartwright. "Mr. Winthrop, I'm sure glad you made it!"

A few minutes later everything was settled. The new captain of the good ship *Argos* was Blake Winthrop. And from Mr. Cartwright's they drove directly to the harbor so that the children could go for a sail.

"You come, too," Blake urged his mother and father, but they smiled and shook their heads.

"I have to do some work, and I'll need your mother's help for a while. Besides, I think the first cruise should be just you kids. This afternoon we'll all have a sail together."

Mr. McGill appeared from the boat shop, and when he heard the news he danced a sailor's jig.

"Hot diggetty!" he cried, and slapped Blake on the back. "Go to it, boy!"

Susie could not remember when she had ever been as happy. This was a special happiness, the happiness of achieving something. Blake had his boat, and she had helped him get it. They were all proud of her, and she loved them all so much now that she even loved Cape Cod, too. She knew now that if you tried to be brave even when you were scared, you soon found out that some of the things that scared you were not as bad as they seemed.

Five minutes later, Uncle Gurney and Aunt Sally and Mr. McGill were watching from the shore as the big mainsail of the *Argos* filled and the boat began to move.

With shouts of delight, the children waved to them.

"Look what's propped up on the rail," chuckled Uncle Gurney. "They certainly can't call her Susie Sneakers any more."

For, crossed on the rail, their toes wiggling blissfully, were Susie's bare feet.

Scott Corbett's introduction to salt water took place on the West Coast. He was eight years old and living near Tacoma, Washington. Although the sea was the peaceful Pacific, "it seemed to rise in the air, out in front of me, like the side of a vast ball," he says. "It scared me."

From Washington Mr. Corbett moved to Kansas City, where he attended high school and junior college. His first literary sale was a parody poem purchased by *College Humor* for six dollars. It was written on a streetcar between class and a job as page in the public library. Later, while a senior at the University of Missouri, he sold "Postscripts" to the *Saturday Evening Post*, thus handily adding to his pocket money.

Mr. Corbett served with the army in Europe and did a stint as *Yank* editor in Paris. In 1951, by then a confirmed salt-water man, he moved to Cape Cod. He had spent several vacations there but actually knew very little about it. Then he and his family decided to buy a house which suddenly became available in East Dennis. "All we knew was that it seemed right for us—and it was."

Now the Corbetts and their eleven-year-old daughter are permanent Cape Cod residents. They enjoy clamming, quahoging, fishing, and just exploring the sandy beaches. Mr. Corbett is also the author of *We Chose Cape Cod*.